REVIEWS OF MICHAEL Z. LEWIN'S AL

EYE OPENER

"...It's an emotional roller coaster-- bemused ch horrified gasps--but it's not to be missed."

Wes Lukowsky, *The American Library Association*

CALLED BY A PANTHER (Winner of a "Marlowe" in Germany)

"...so amusing, the wonder is that it also works so well as a thriller... Fast, funny and brilliant."

Tom Nolan, *The Wall Street Journal*

OUT OF SEASON

"...[Ross] Macdonald followers who want to switch will find Lewin devises more intricate plots and peoples them with more interesting characters... They're going to enjoy Lewin's way of giving even the most minor of characters vivid and unstereotyped personalities."

Tony Hillerman, *Washington Post Book World*

MISSING WOMAN (Adapted for television in Japan)

"Sharp style, crisp dialogue, believable characters."

New York Times Book Review Critic's Choice for 1981

THE SILENT SALESMAN

"...literate and funny, smooth, exciting and tight-paced."

Margaret Manning, *Boston Globe*

THE ENEMIES WITHIN

"Lewin has brains and style, and that's why the story is such a good one."

Dorothy B. Hughes, *Los Angeles Times*

THE WAY WE DIE NOW

"Lewin writes with style and sensibility and wit. He has a fine poetic sense of detail that lights up every page. He can frighten the reader too."

Ross Macdonald

ASK THE RIGHT QUESTION (Edgar nominated)

"Characters are finely drawn, plotting is logical, details are well worked out. You can be sure that we'll be seeing more of Mr. Samson."

New York Times Book Review

Other books by Michael Z. Lewin

Albert Samson series

ASK THE RIGHT QUESTION
THE WAY WE DIE NOW
THE ENEMIES WITHIN
THE SILENT SALESMAN
MISSING WOMAN
OUT OF SEASON (OUT OF TIME in UK)
CALLED BY A PANTHER
EYE OPENER

Leroy Powder Trilogy

NIGHT COVER
HARD LINE
LATE PAYMENTS

Other Indianapolis novels

OUTSIDE IN
AND BABY WILL FALL (CHILD PROOF in UK)
UNDERDOG
OH JOE

Lunghi Family Trilogy

FAMILY BUSINESS
FAMILY PLANNING
FAMILY WAY

Other novels

CUTTING LOOSE
CONFESSIONS OF A DISCONTENTED DEITY

Short stories

TELLING TAILS
ROVER'S TALES
THE RELUCTANT DETECTIVE and Other Stories
FAMILY TRIO

Non Fiction

HOW TO BEAT COLLEGE TESTS:
A Guide to Ease the Burden of Useless Courses

ALIEN QUARTET

ALBERT SAMSON STORIES

MICHAEL Z. LEWIN

iUniverse®

ALIEN QUARTET
ALBERT SAMSON STORIES

Cover design by Tristan Buckland
www.tristanbuckland.com

iUniverse books may be ordered through booksellers or by contacting:

iUniverse
1663 Liberty Drive
Bloomington, IN 47403
www.iuniverse.com
1-800-Authors (1-800-288-4677)

ISBN: 978-1-5320-6109-7 (sc)
ISBN: 978-1-5320-6110-3 (e)

Print information available on the last page.

iUniverse rev. date: 11/02/2018

This book is for my beloved Liza Cody
who helped the writing of each story in innumerable ways.
I made her dinner last night to thank her, yet again.

CONTENTS

WHO I AM

He seemed normal enough. Except, of course, for the fact that he had come to consult a private detective. "Welcome," I said, as I opened the door.

My visitor was in his mid-twenties. He said, "Thank you," as he crossed my threshold. We were off to a famous start. I like people with manners.

His plain blue shirt and dark blue slacks almost amounted to overdressing, given that it was unseasonably hot for late September. Did he want to make a good impression, like visiting a doctor or a lawyer? Why not? A lot of times a PI can give more pain relief than other professionals.

I gestured to my Client's Chair, the only furniture that has accompanied me to each new office around Indianapolis over the years. He sat. Where so several had sat before.

My visitor looked to be an average guy – medium build, medium height, medium amount of medium-brown hair. I said, "I'm Albert Samson, but I expect you guessed that from the sign outside."

"Which also says you're an investigator."

"And you are…?"

"LeBron James." When I raised an eyebrow he added, "But not the famous one."

Given that he was white and considerably shorter than six-eight I'd worked that much out for myself. "So is that your given name or are you a rabid basketball fan?"

"No." He tilted his head with a smile. "And in a way."

I began to wonder how much time to give "LeBron."

"You're wondering if I'm a nutter," he said.

"Yup."

He laughed. Which was reassuring, because not many real nutters laugh at themselves.

I said, "I'm also wondering what kind of help you've come to me for."

"And whether I can pay for it."

"That too."

From a pocket he pulled a roll of golden yellow paper. The roll opened into a stack and he began to count. "You do accept astros, don't you? The current exchange rate is one-to-one with US dollars. A thousand will be enough to get you started, won't it?"

He pushed the pile of "astro" notes my way. They were Monopoly money, hundreds, with a letter A stamped in the upper left hand corner.

"It's the official seal that makes them a bona-fide currency," he said.

I pushed them back. "My bank and I are on the narrow-minded side when it comes to cash."

"No wonder our country's finances are in chaos." Shaking his head slowly, he restored the astros to his bankroll.

"Mr James—" I began.

"My time is running out."

"Quickly."

From another pocket he pulled a roll of the more familiar green. Again he peeled off ten hundreds. "Society should be open to astros. It's a fully supported currency, which is more than dollars are, the way the government is printing money."

I didn't ask what astros were supported by. He would have told me.

He pushed the new pile across the desk. "Will that be enough for you to hear me out?"

"If they're real and if they're yours to spend."

"I'm not crazy, Mr Samson."

"I'm glad to hear it."

"I am, however, an alien."

I sighed.

"You're surprised," he said. "And you're wondering what I mean. Whether I mean I'm from Timbuktu or something."

I held one of the hundreds up to the light. It looked real to me. So it bought a few more minutes. "What do you mean you're an alien, Mr James? Are you from Timbuktu or something?"

"My father was an extra-terrestrial."

"So are you saying you're half-alien? Or was your mother from Timbuktu? Which would make you doubly alien, but not fully alien in the species sense."

"My mother's from Santa Claus."

"I'm getting *very* tired here."

"You must have heard of the town, Santa Claus."

A southern Indiana hamlet that officially adopted the name "Santa Claus" in the middle of the 19th Century… "OK, your mother's from Santa Claus and your father was an extra-terrestrial."

"Now you've got it. But alien genetics are dominant, not recessive."

"By which you're trying to say that your father's half rules. Does that mean that you are blessed – or cursed – with special powers?"

"Not ones I can demonstrate like party tricks. It's more an ability to empathize."

Perhaps he was pushing me to call him loony and kick him out. But the truth was if he wanted to be an alien, he was a housetrained alien who said thank you and put hundred-dollar bills on my desk.

"You said your father *was* an alien… Does that mean he's dead?"

"He went back," LeBron said.

"To?"

"Mom doesn't know the name of the planet."

"He never writes, he never calls?"

He smiled patiently. "Now you're making fun of me."

"By laying your parentage on the table alongside your astros you're challenging me to make fun of you. Since I can't be the first person you've done your origin riffs for, I'm sure you've experienced unsympathetic, doubting or even aggressive responses. Whereas I am merely being humorous, killing time until you decide to tell me what – on earth – you've come here for."

"You're right, of course."

"About…?"

"The responses I've had to my singularity."

"Singularity? You think you're the only mixed-species alien around?"

"You're right again. I don't believe that I am unique any more than that the human race is the only intelligent life form in the universe. I just haven't ever met anyone like me."

"I have things to do, Mr James. It is now time to tell me just what kind of bang you want for your thousand bucks."

"My house was burgled yesterday."

"What was taken?"

"Several things, but the most important was a precious stone artifact. Well, precious to me. About the size of my hand."

He held up his hand. It was medium.

"The stone is oval although the edges aren't smooth. There's a groove down the center with shorter grooves branching out on both sides."

"And this stone, it's precious because it's ancient, or what?"

"The marks on it are my father's handprint."

"Ah."

"Mom said he made it specially for me. He put his hand flat on a piece of limestone and he closed his eyes and after a minute the grooves were there."

He looked at me, expecting comment. I looked again at the hundred-dollar bills.

"He told Mom to give it to me when I turned seventeen – that's an important age where he comes from. He told her that he made it so he could touch me."

"*Touch* you?"

"I first held it on my birthday and I felt… electrified – that's the best word – electrified from the moment I took it in my hands. I've felt the same again whenever I've touched it."

The question now was how touched my new client actually was. But I didn't ask it.

"You're thinking I'm crazy again."

It took more self-awareness for him to ask that. Was self-awareness a super-power? "Are you suggesting the thief might electrocute himself by touching this stone of yours?"

"I don't know what effect it will have on other people. Only Mom and I have ever held it and she says she's never put her hand over the grooves."

"Do you have a picture, or a drawing?"

LeBron took a small photograph from his shirt pocket. It showed, yes, a stone with grooves a bit like the veins of a maple leaf. "Your father's handprint?"

"Mom says 'hand' isn't quite right, but it is the imprint of the end of the limb that functions for Dad the way human hands function for us."

I said, "Tell me about the robbery."

"Yesterday I went out for a walk a little after three. When I came back an hour later someone had broken in and taken the stone. I keep it on my desk on a small velvet cushion."

"And when you noticed it was missing…?"

"I saw that other things were gone too. Then I discovered marks on my back door. Like with a chisel."

"How secure was your back door?"

"A Yale lock. Maybe I should have gotten a Harvard."

A joke. I was warming to this Indy ET. "What else was taken?"

He produced a list. "Mostly CDs and DVDs but a small radio shaped like a flower is missing too – before you ask, it's from Ayres, not my father."

"Computer? Television?"

"No."

About thirty items were on the list – all small and portable. One, however, caught my eye. "A DVD of 'The Sound of Music'?"

"The 40th anniversary collector's edition."

"You… didn't strike me as a Sound of Music kind of guy."

"Everybody loves The Sound of Music."

I raised my eyebrows.

"You think I should watch 'Star Trek' or 'Battlestar Galactica'?"

"I lack imagination," I said. "What value – in dollars – would you put on the stolen items?"

"To replace new? Maybe five hundred."

"You're spending a thousand to replace five hundred?"

"I'm spending it to get back what's irreplaceable."

"Have you called the police?"

"No."

"They're free, unlike me."

"They're also small-minded and intolerant."

Though my best friend used to be a policeman and my daughter was one now, I said, "You've had some bad experiences?"

He nodded.

Considering what cops have to deal with routinely, I could see that most wouldn't have much patience for "singularity." I said, "I'll need to take a look at your back door."

"Fine."

"Any idea who might have done this?"

"There's a neighbor who doesn't like me."

"Why not?"

"I'm new. Everyone else in the neighborhood has been there a long time."

"You're integrating the area for mixed-species aliens?"

"I know you don't take me seriously. Shall we just take that as read and move on?"

"Sorry," I said, meaning it. "You were away from the house for about an hour between three and four. Are you always out then?"

"Often, but not always."

"Have you found signs of an attempt to break in before?"

"No."

"Tell me about the neighbor who doesn't like you."

"She calls me names when we pass in the street."

"Such as?"

"Weirdo. Sicko."

"How did she form this opinion of you?"

"I went to her house for dinner a week after I moved in."

"She invited you to dinner?"

"It was a neighborly thing."

"Let me guess. Over the meatloaf you explained about your singularity?"

"It's who I am," LeBron James said.

2

I sent my client home and promised to follow after a few errands. The first was a visit to my bank. I wanted confirmation that his dollars weren't homemade like the astros. But a teller took eight of the hundreds with a smile. So I called myself Me Of Little Faith and went for some lunch.

I live above Bud's Dugout, a luncheonette. Bud was my father and, like LeBron's dad, long ago he left this world for another. My mother owns it now and frequently feeds me. I carried Today's Special to a window table and settled to thinking about how I'd find a handprint. Other than on a hand.

The thief forced a door and stole small saleable items. That suggested an opportunist who minimized his, or her, time in LeBron's house. But why take the stone? What value could someone who stole a Deluxe Sound of Music DVD think it had? And who would he plan to sell it to? Or she.

However, maybe the handprint wasn't taken because of its cash value. Maybe the thief took it *because* of its value to LeBron. If so a random crime morphed into a vengeful one where the thief knew who he was stealing from. Or she.

So, a random incident or a purposeful one? I called my daughter. Why? Because she is po-lice.

"I'm on duty, Dad," Sam said.

"But you answered your phone."

"I don't like private calls unless it's an emergency." Sam is in her probationary period as an Indy cop. She still likes to go by the book. "Is Grandma OK?"

"This isn't an emergency, but it is work. I have a client from the Beechport area whose house was burgled yesterday. I need to know if there've been other break-ins over there recently."

"And just why would a patrol officer on the northwest know about that?"

"Because she's razor sharp and absorbs information that passes before her on the endless pieces of paper distributed by police HQ." When she didn't respond to this I added, "Or she might know someone who would know."

"I'm *not* going to feed you police information the way Uncle Jerry did." My best friend retired from the force about the time Sam joined up.

"I helped his career more than once, honey."

"Call Southeast Sector HQ. Help their careers." She ended the call.

Children are so ungrateful these days.

3

LeBron's house was modest for a guy carrying rolls of hundreds in his pockets – one storey, white frame, not large and it had seen better days. Wooden steps led to a porch and one of the columns that held up its roof had a hole the size of a grapefruit where the wood had rotted. Decay that might not be so visible made me step carefully.

LeBron answered the bell quickly and ushered me inside.

Although the exterior was down-at-heel, the house interior was elegant and plush. It had been opened into a single large area. Poles bore the weight of absent walls. The remaining walls were painted as large pictures, ranging from a Mediterranean seaside to a pattern in plaid. The poles were decorated too, looking more like strange growths springing from below than anything suitable for firemen or naked dancers.

The few items of furniture looked carefully chosen and placed. "Amazing," I said to my client.

"Good amazing or bad amazing?"

Was he soliciting a compliment? "Did you do all this work yourself?"

"You think an alien will be impractical and have no eye?"

"I just asked, Mr James."

"I trained as a carpenter," he said.

I strolled around. The work was solid and finely finished. Not to everybody's taste but… "Good amazing."

"I'm glad you didn't just say it's 'different.'"

"Although it is."

"I mean the way people here use the word. They say, "That's different,' when they mean they'd set it on fire given half a chance. They probably said, 'That's different,' when they first saw pasta."

"I love pasta, Mr James."

"What I meant—"

"Show me your backdoor, please."

We went to the back of the house. No porch, just concrete steps leading down from a concrete stoop. Fresh marks in the wood showed where the door had been prised open. They were narrow, perhaps made with a chisel or a broad screwdriver. But the door was poorly hung in the first place.

"I grant you," I said, "this door was forced open, but I doubt it took much force."

"The wood's not very good."

"You're not concerned about security?"

"I thought thieves wouldn't bother with a place that looks rundown."

"Some burglars target shabby houses *because* there won't be much security."

Shaking his head slowly he said, "That's sad."

"What are you? A do-gooder?"

"I'm working on it."

Next I had him show me where things had been taken from. The DVDs and CDs struck me as easily spotted by a burglar with a knapsack and ten minutes to spare. And the handprint might have caught a larcenous eye because of its velvet cushion, now sitting empty on a large oak desk was close to LeBron's entertainment equipment.

But, conversely, the discs *might* have been taken to cover up the theft of the handprint.

"Who knows about your father's handprint, LeBron?" He hesitated so I became more specific. "Where were you when your mother gave it to you?"

"In her house."

"And did you leave it in the house, or show it off, or what?"

"I kept it in my room."

"Do you have siblings? Or half-siblings?"

"I am my mother's only child."

"So who besides your mother might know about the handprint?"

"No one, I don't think."

"It wasn't written up in the local paper? Your mother didn't tell her friends about it?"

"Mom doesn't have many friends." Then, "No, we didn't talk to people about it."

New tack. I said, "Who has been inside the house since you moved here?"

"No one."

"*No* one. Not your mother? Come up to see you settled?"

"Mom doesn't have a car." He took a deep breath. "She's in a hospital. She has a condition." I waited for him to continue. He said, "She has an illness. And, no, before you ask, it's not a mental one. Although it has defied identification by medical science."

"Defied?"

"The doctors can't explain it. She is photophobic, she's lost her hair and she's put extra muscle on her arms and legs. *I* think it may be something she got inadvertently from my father."

"An interstellar STD?"

"I'm getting fed up with your disrespect, Mr Samson."

"You challenge me – and presumably other people – to 'disrespect' you, Mr *James*. But if you don't like the way I think and talk then fire me now. Otherwise just take a semi-alien deep breath and answer any damn questions I choose to ask you. Because I am doing my damnedest to find your alien rock, as well as your DVDs and CDs."

It took him several seconds to say, "Yeah. All right. Sorry."

"Is 'sorry' not a word you use very often?"

"Perhaps not often enough."

"So maybe you're not so atypical for a human male after all."

"Maybe."

"What name was on your birth certificate, Mr James?"

More seconds. "Curtis Nelson."

"Was a father named on the certificate?"

"No." He looked uncomfortable but he was giving me direct answers.

I had real sympathy for my client. No matter how he chose to tell his backstory or the name he'd answer to, he was clearly one of life's outsiders. He and I weren't twins but I don't fit in Hoosierdom's round holes either.

I said, "So, your mother hasn't been inside this room. Anybody else? Friends?"

His face told me that his Facebook was a blank page.

"Neighbors? Gas and electricity? Jehovah's Witnesses? Welcome wagon?"

"Both my immediate neighbors came to the front door."

"Including…" I checked my notes. "Eileen Simberley, who calls you names?"

"She brought me some peach cobbler the day after I arrived."

"Neighborly. Did you invite her in?"

"No."

"Why not?"

"The house wasn't fit for guests."

"How was the peach cobbler?" When he hesitated, I said, "You *did* eat it, didn't you?"

"I don't much like sweet things."

"Now you *are* talking like an alien."

"I tasted it. It was fine. I put the rest in a compost heap I started in the backyard. I cleaned the dish and took it back to her."

"Did you put it on her porch, ring the bell, and run?"

"I knocked, Mr Samson. I may be an alien but I believe in manners."

I like manners too, but I don't always have them. Bad Albert. "So what happened when she answered the door?"

"She thanked me for the dish. I told her it was a nice thing for her to do. And…"

"She invited you to dinner, you went a week later, told her what you are, and she's been treating you badly ever since?"

"I told her *who* I *am*, Mr Samson."

"So you can compromise enough to thank her for peach cobbler but not enough to hold back on the alien stuff until a second date?"

"It was hardly a 'date'. Although her son, Willy, didn't eat with us." Something else came into his mind as he thought about dinner with his neighbor.

"What?"

"There… It was embarrassing." I waited. "She tried to kiss me."

"And you're not that kind of alien?"

"I thought… I didn't think… We were sitting on the couch. I was talking about my plans for a center for people who nobody else wants. The homeless, the addicts, the alcoholics, the dispossessed. And she said I was talking too much."

"And she kissed you."

"Yes."

"What happened then?"

"She said she wouldn't mind about the age gap if I didn't. But I said I didn't think of her that way and… Well…"

"You ran for it?"

"Pretty much."

"And she's been treating you badly ever since."

"Pretty much."

"And did your other neighbor make a pass at you too?"

"Mrs Frickart? Heavens no."

"But she came to your door?"

"She brought me a macaroni cheese."

"What a nice neighborhood. And what did *she* invite you to?"

"Nothing, but we do talk occasionally, porch to porch. She's sweet. And very physically fit for her age."

"Which is?"

He shook his head.

"Twenty, forty, sixty, eighty or a hundred?"

"Sixty?"

"And the neighbors across the street? What did they bring you?"

"I've never met them, or anyone else around here."

"And has *nobody* been inside this house? Not even to deliver timber or piping or furniture?"

"Oh, the furniture. But that was a month ago. It all came in the course of one week, once I'd finished the basic layout."

"Any cross words?"

"None at all. They were good. Careful. Respectful."

"So nobody has been inside your house since you finished redecorating?"

"Not until yesterday. You are the first person I've *invited* in."

4

Eileen Simberley's house wasn't a twin of LeBron's but it might have been a cousin. However it appeared to be in much better repair. Not a rotting hole to be seen.

I pushed the doorbell. After a minute, I pushed it again. Then I knocked.

This produced a resident but not Eileen Simberley unless she was in her teens and a boy. The son, Willy, I presumed.

"What?" His manner wasn't aggressive, just impatient as if I'd interrupted what he was doing. Fair enough.

"Is Eileen Simberley here, please?"

"No. You want to leave a message?"

"Can you say when she'll be back?"

"She won't buy nothing."

"And I won't sell nothing."

He thought for a moment. "What's it about, mister?"

"It's about a burglary that took place next door yesterday."

"You a cop?"

"You a criminal?"

He frowned. "Next door where? Mr and Mrs Hall or the weirdo?"

"The weirdo. There was a break-in. Several things were stolen."

"And you think Mom did it? You're the crazy one now."

"Not everyone I talk to is a suspect. Maybe she saw something that might help me find out what happened."

"When yesterday?"

"Between about three and four in the afternoon."

"Broad daylight? Wow."

I was interested by his Wow. "So where were *you* yesterday afternoon?"

"Ain't you supposed to have a responsible adult present when you question a minor?"

"Is that a confession?"

"No."

"You prefer to commit your burglaries at night?"

"If you seen my record then you seen I don't do that anymore."

"What do you do instead?"

"I sell stuff on eBay."

"Stolen stuff?"

"No. *Jeez.*"

"Is that what you were just doing? Putting things on eBay?"

"We call it 'listing' them. And, yeah, as it happens, I was."

"Shouldn't you be in school?"

He coughed twice. "I'm sick."

"Sick a lot?"

He coughed again. "I'm chronic."

"Are you old enough to sell things on eBay?"

"I sell things for Mom."

"What kind of things?"

"If you want to bid you can go to her site."

"Or you could just show me what she's selling at the moment."

He wasn't eager. "Shouldn't you have a search warrant?"

"Maybe I'll buy something. Save you the postage and packing."

He gave in to what he seemed to think was inevitable and led me into a living room. It took up most of the side of the house that faced LeBron's. Between two windows a computer sat on a table. A small scale, packing tape, envelopes, bits of cardboard, bubble wrap, and rolls of wrapping paper sat next to the computer. There was also a stack of yellow t-shirts.

Next to the table two rows of metal shelves stretched out toward the back of the house. They were full of *stuff*.

"These are what I'm listing now." The boy pointed to the t-shirts.

But I ignored them and walked among the shelves. Mostly they bore clothes, neatly folded with labels that gave a size and weight. But there were a lot of small items too. I riffled through the DVDs. Not a Sound of Music to be seen.

I asked, "Where's it all come from?"

"Mom gets it a lot of places. I do the listing. Each thing, I take its picture and weigh it and put the price she says to sell it at. When someone buys something I pack it up."

I pointed to the t-shirts. "May I?"

He nodded.

I unfolded one. It read, "Keep America Beautiful: don't let white boys on the dance floor."

"Five bucks to you. It'll be eight if you buy it off us on eBay."

"Yellow's not my color. Sorry." I handed him the shirt and he refolded it like he'd been folding t-shirts all his life. I wondered how long that life had been. He didn't look sixteen yet. I said, "Were you here yesterday afternoon?"

"What of it?"

"You might have seen someone hanging around the weirdo's house. Or heard something. Or seen something strange."

"I don't look out the windows much," he said.

"OK. When's your mother coming back?"

He scratched his head in front of an ear. "Could be anytime. She just went out for some cigs. I keep telling her it's a dirty habit."

"But it doesn't make her a bad person," I said.

He smiled. "Naw, Mom's a good person. Mostly."

"That's about all you can expect from anybody." I stuck out my hand. "I'm Albert."

"Willy." We shook.

"Laters," I said, and left.

5

Mrs Frickart, the neighbor on the other side of LeBron, answered her door in sweats. "Hang on." She held up a hand and studied a wrist. After a moment she wrote something in a notebook. "OK, got it. What can I do for you, sonny?"

When I looked curious she said, "Pulse rate."

"If I'm interrupting I can come back later."

"I'm doing a circuit but my heart'll still be there in ten minutes. You wanna come in?"

I followed her into a room dotted with homemade exercise equipment – weights made from water-filled plastic cartons, buckets of sand, broom handles, and things I didn't understand but was afraid to ask about.

Maybe I shouldn't have been surprised, in this fitness-conscious age, but Mrs Frickart was about five feet tall, perhaps seventy years old, and was carrying all the spare weight of a jockey. Which made me heightist, ageist and weightist. Running and lifting weights have never appealed to me nearly as much as standing still and leaving heavy things where they are.

Mrs Frickart read the surprise on my face. "What?" she said. "You think I should spend my retirement making pies for grandchildren who already carry too high a percentage of body fat?"

"I think they're lucky to have such a fine role model in this sugary and saturated fatty world."

"Care to guess how old I am?"

"No."

"How about my resting pulse?"

"Forty for both?"

She chuckled. "You'd benefit from some training yourself, sonny. How long's your waist been that big? I hire out as a trainer."

"I bet I couldn't afford you."

"Well, if you can rewire houses we could make a deal."

"I can barely put up Christmas lights."

"Well, just don't leave it too late," she said, sounding very much like my mother all of a sudden. "So what is it you want?"

"I'm investigating a burglary that took place next door yesterday afternoon."

"At the spaceman's? Really? In the afternoon?"

"Yes, yes and yes."

"Jeez, poor guy."

"Were you home yesterday afternoon?"

"Part of it. You're going to ask which part now, aren't you? Well let me think on that one." She put a fist under her chin and looked reflective. "Yesterday I ran so I'd have aimed to be back in time for Patsy. That's my granddaughter, who comes to me after school every day except Monday. Her mom only just moved back to Indy and Pats stays here till my Honey finishes at work."

"What happens Mondays?"

"Computer Club, so Honey gets her from school. But on my running days I'm back by three-thirty, though I leave the door open just in case I'm held up."

"You leave the door open?"

"Not open wide with a sign saying House Clearance. Just unlocked. Get real, sonny."

"Even so, you're not worried about burglars?"

"This is a good neighborhood."

"And you get along with the spaceman?"

"The spaceman's a pussycat. He could even be fun, if he'd loosen up. He'd enjoy life more with some regular CV work"

"Have you told him that?"

"Sure. We talk when we're setting out sometimes. I been doing that with neighbors all my life. You care to guess how many years I've been living in this house?"

"Too many for my fingers and toes, I bet. So were you back by three-thirty yesterday?"

"You know, I *was* a few minutes late. I saw this guy beating on a stray dog in an alley. I couldn't just run past that like it was a chocodile, now could I?"

"How late were you?"

"Nine past four. Pats was inside, already at the computer."

"You know to the minute?"

"Two-twenty-eight to four-oh-nine. I'd check my run folder, but I remember it now, because of the delay."

"So Patsy might have seen something going on next door between the time she got here and a bit past four?"

"She didn't say, but I didn't ask. And I gotta say, she's not the most *aware* child. She comes in and goes straight to that machine. I tell her exercise would make her brain work better in front of that screen, but she just figures it's Memaw on the con."

"Suspicious of Memaw, is she?"

"Kids her age are too suspicious of older people and too trusting of the young ones, if you ask me."

"How old is she?"

"Thirteen. Fourteen in a month."

"Is it OK if I come back later to ask Patsy if she saw anything yesterday?"

"Sure. And meanwhile will you go for a run or would you rather stay here and use my weights?"

"Now why would Patsy ever think her Memaw could be on the con, Mrs F?"

6

I did get some exercise after leaving Mrs Frickart, just not the running kind. Instead I walked the alley behind my client's house. Alleys symbolize what's behind the façades of a row of houses but as well as look I wanted time to think a bit about the case's core question: Why would a burglar take a chunk of limestone with some grooves cut in it?

It was hard to imagine what commercial value a thief could think it might have. None of what was taken was of high value, but even visualizing a smalltime thief offering bargains in a bar I couldn't guess what he would claim the "handprint" actually *was.* Or she.

I strolled slowly up the alley until I got to the back of LeBron's house. The perp had entered by the back door. Was that because he or she *knew* a lot of people were home in the afternoon in this neighborhood? Or just standard burglar etiquette?

In fact the back of LeBron's didn't provide much shelter from neighborly eyes. The few fences along the alley were low. The trees and shrubs were scattered. Most houses had pull-in spaces for their vehicles rather than garages. It was a well-established neighborhood but not a prosperous one.

Even the boundary lines between properties weren't always clear. Maybe good fences only make good neighbors closer to downtown. These folks appeared comfortable being part of a joined-up community.

Except for whoever had robbed LeBron. The break-in seemed at odds with the neighborhood atmosphere. Unless it was driven by a feeling that LeBron was out of place here.

After the alley I walked around a couple of nearby blocks. LeBron's immediate neighborhood was much like the rest in the area. When I got back to his street it was after three. Still early for Patsy, but maybe Willy's mother was back.

I paused on the sidewalk in front of the Simberleys'. I saw no cars parked on the street that weren't there when I interrupted Willy the first time. And the space at the back of the house was still empty too. So my bet was that Eileen Simberley hadn't returned from wherever she went to get her cigarettes.

I lost.

The door opened and a wiry blonde woman appeared in the frame. "Hey," she called.

I headed up the path. "Eileen Simberley?"

"Was it you that interrogated my son without an adult being present?"

"I asked him when you'd be home."

"And a bunch of other things. That's illegal. I could have your badge." She waved a finger at me.

"You're not going to get my badge, Mrs Simberley."

"Don't mess with me, pal."

"I need to ask you some questions. I don't *want* to make trouble, for you or your truanting son, so can we get my questions out of the way now, and here?" Like with dog-whispering, sometimes you need to show firmness whether you feel it or not.

Eileen Simberley grimaced but then she stepped onto the porch. "Not much I can do about it, I guess."

I didn't run through her other options. She marked my silence by lighting up a cigarette.

I don't automatically class smokers as bad people. Even my girlfriend these days is a smoking recidivist. But Eileen Simberley didn't offer me one. That's plain bad manners.

"Sit," I said, pointing to the top step.

Without comment she sat. "Willy says it's about the freak next door."

I sat too. "Why do you say he's a freak?"

She stared and tightened one cheek in a sneer. "Do you *know* him?"

"Seems like a nice enough guy."

"Has he spun you the tale about his daddy?"

"Yes."

"And isn't that *asking* to be called a freak?"

"He says he's different from most people, true."

"Well there you are." She inhaled deeply and blew a lot of smoke, all of it in my direction.

"In some cultures," I said, "a person's being different is a positive thing."

"Well, this here isn't one of those cultures."

She wasn't wrong about that. I'm no spaceman's child but I've spent a lifetime on the edges of what folks around here call normal. However I wasn't here as Eileen Simberley's tolerance outreach worker. I said, "My job is to find out what happened yesterday afternoon."

"Willy says someone robbed the freak's house."

"Did you already know about that?"

"How would *I* know?"

"Maybe you did it. Or asked a friend to take some things to show your neighbor he's unwelcome."

"You have no call to accuse me of that."

"You say nasty things whenever you see him."

"Told you about that, did he?" She sucked and smoked again. "Well, I didn't do any such thing."

"Maybe you saw a stranger hanging around."

"Other than you?"

"You didn't see me here yesterday afternoon."

"*Are* you a stranger? Foreign or something? Should I call the cops?"

"Doesn't the subject of neighborhood security concern you?"

"'Course it does. But we never had a problem, not until that freak moved in."

"Did something happen before yesterday? Break-ins? Other crimes?"

She wagged her head from side-to-side. Uncharitably I wondered if she was trying to shake a memory out. "No. But it was only a matter of time."

"Why?"

"You drop a weirdo into a nice, quiet neighborhood and it's going to upset things."

"Drop a stone in a pond and the ripples soon fade away."

"You ask me, it's the weirdo that oughta fade away. There must be someplace better for him and his center to 'help' the druggies and dropouts."

"Somebody else caused the problem this time, Mrs Simberley. He didn't steal stuff from himself."

"You sure?" More smoke. "Didn't think of that, did you? Because a lot of these freaky guys, they do things just for the attention. Look, all I'm saying is that a guy who makes an oddball out of himself, a guy who's into crazy alien stuff like that, he could do anything and it wouldn't surprise me. In fact, if Willy wasn't big enough to take care of himself, I'd worry – you know, *worry* – about that guy being next door. And I'd be a hell of a lot happier anyways if he just went somewheres else."

"Where were you yesterday afternoon between three and four, Mrs Simberley?"

"In and out, I expect. I don't keep track."

I fixed her eyes and waited.

"I was out, getting some stock."

"To sell on eBay?"

"You want a nice shirt? I got a couple that would be a lot more flattering than what you got on now."

"How do you get your stock?"

"Why do you want to know?"

I waited. I preferred her to work out that what she said might support her alibi. Especially since I was already in slippery territory because of her presumption that I was a cop.

"I get my stuff a lot of different ways." Smoke. "Like... Like, did you know that out at the airport, a lot of people don't claim their luggage?"

"Really?"

"Over a year, lots of bags get left behind. The airport tries to trace the owners but even with all their computers some bags just don't get claimed. They sell the unclaimed luggage off and one of the things I do is buy bags and sell what I find inside."

"And is that what were you doing yesterday? Between three and four?"

"All right, all right. I was with my friend, Carlo. You know. *With* him."

"He'd confirm that, would he?"

"If he had to." She smoked. "Willy's home so much... It makes it hard."

"OK."

"OK? No address for Carlo or nothing?"

"I believe you."

"Just like that? You don't want Carlo's address or phone."

"What I want is to ask Willy a few more questions."

She shrugged, got up, and pitched her butt into the grass. I followed her inside.

Willy was at the computer. He gave it another minute of concentration and then looked surprised when he saw me. “What’s *he* doing here, Ma?”

“He’s got some questions. About the weirdo.”

I faced them both. “I need straight answers, now. Did either of you see any strangers in the vicinity of your neighbor’s house yesterday afternoon?”

Eileen Simberley said, “No.” Willy glanced at his mother before he said the same.

“Did either of you see someone you knew, not a stranger, in the vicinity of his house yesterday?”

“Other than him?” Willy asked.

“Other than him.”

“I didn’t. Ma?”

Eileen Simberley shook her head.

I gave each of them a stare. But I believed them. “OK,” I said to her. “You said you have shirts that might be good for me.”

Willy said, “Ma?”

“Those white oxfords you put on day before yesterday.”

Willy looked to the array of shelves.

I said, “Just tell me what to search for and I’ll check them out online. I’m not looking to cut corners or get a freebie.”

“Simplest thing is to look up my Seller page on eBay… Do you use eBay?”

“I can learn.”

“Go to eBay dot com and look up how to find a particular seller. I’m ‘Indygirl329’.”

“329?”

“There are a lot of girls in this town. You’d probably know that if you were younger and dressed better.”

7

Memaw Frickart opened the door before I got up to her porch. "You're back."

I wiped my brow with a sleeve to suggest I'd been running.

"Eileen Simberley wore you out?"

There was a lot of keeping-track-from-behind-the-curtains in this neighborhood… "Absolutely exhausted me."

"Some would say she's known for it," she said with a smile, "but I couldn't possibly comment. Well, come on in. Patsy's here. I told her you want to talk." In the hallway shadows I saw a sandy-haired girl six inches taller than her grandmother and probably twice the weight. I waved to her.

No response. However Mrs Frickart gestured me toward the living room. "Find yourself some space. Care for some carrot juice, Mr…"

"Samson. But thank you, no."

"Pats?"

"I *don't* think so," Patsy said. "You got any soda?"

"I *don't* think so," Mrs Frickart said, duplicating her tone. They both laughed. It was evidence of a nice relationship.

Patsy followed me into the room. I said, "Hi," and offered a hand. "I'm Albert."

After hesitating, she touched her fingers lightly on mine, a minimalist handshake. "Hi."

We settled at opposite ends of a couch in the living *cum* exercise room. Two sandbags shared a cushion between us.

"So you come here often, I understand."

Patsy's eyes widened. Then she covered her mouth.

"What?" I said.

"That sounds like a pick-up line." She blushed.

"Get picked up often?" I let her have a moment of teenage anguish about how to respond before I said, "Sorry, but you know what I meant. You come here most afternoons after school."

"Yeah."

"And school… It's high school?"

"Yeah."

"What year are you?"

"Freshman. I just started at Southern."

It was late September so she'd only have been there for a few weeks. "Do you like it?"

"It's OK. Hot, though."

"Must be the Midwestern Warming."

She blinked and then smiled as she got my "joke". "Uh huh."

"Getting to know people there?"

She shrugged. "Not much yet."

"Where were you before Indy?"

"Lexington." Then she added, "Kentucky."

"Uh huh."

"Mom and Dad, they…" She shrugged again. "So we came here. But school had already been going for a week when we moved so I'm behind in everything."

And coming from Kentucky had probably isolated her all the more. Hicks from Indiana like to look down on hicks from Kentucky and they don't get hickier than at a high school. "It'll come."

Yet another shrug. "That's what Mom says."

"So she must be very wise. What about people outside of school? You getting to know any of them?"

She frowned, not sure what I was getting at.

"Like," I said, "do you know any of the people in this neighborhood?"

"You mean like the spaceman?"

"Like him."

She shook her head.

"But you'd recognize him?"

She nodded.

"Did you see him yesterday?"

"Yeah, I did. I was on my way here and he walked right past me but he didn't say hello or anything."

"Did you say hello or anything to him?"

"I would have said something if he'd said something to me, even though he is a weirdo."

"Why is he a weirdo?"

After a moment she said, "I heard people talk about him."

"Where?"

"At school."

I tried to be casual. "Who talks about him at school?"

"Willy."

"Willy Simberley?"

A nod. "I don't, like, know him – he's a junior – but he was telling them in Computer Club and I heard."

"Willy goes to Computer Club?"

"Oh yeah. He's great." Another blush. "With computers, I mean."

"I thought he didn't go to school much."

"I heard somebody say he's away a lot of afternoons. But he's been at Computer Club both times I was there."

"What's he good at?"

"Everything. He's, like, a legend. Even the seniors ask him stuff."

"When I talked to him this afternoon he was listing things on eBay for his mother."

"Yeah, but that's child's play. Any idiot can do that."

"Once the idiot knows how."

She tilted her head. "Do you know how?"

"No."

She laughed as Mrs Frickart joined us, carrying a tray.

"She just called me an idiot," I said. "Make her stop."

Patsy laughed again and Mrs F didn't bat an eyelash. "I'm glad you're getting along." She set the tray on a coffee table. There were three glasses on it. One had a small amount of dark orange liquid in it. "That's for you, Mr Samson," she said. "Give it a try. I put a little cilantro in it. Gives it a bit of tang."

"No actual Tang then?"

She laughed but Patsy looked blank. Too young.

"My Pats is a wonderful girl, isn't she?"

What can you say when a grandmother asks that? "She sure is. I was about to ask her to show me how to use eBay."

"Well, if it's on a computer she'll know how to do it."

I looked at Patsy. "Would you mind? If any idiot can do it, I probably qualify."

"Sure," Patsy said. "If it's OK, Memaw."

"Be my guest." She gestured toward a computer on a narrow table well away from her exercise equipment. She gave Patsy a glass of a liquid that looked like lemonade.

I sipped my tangy carrot juice. It tasted like carrot juice, only tangy. Oh, all right. It was good. "This is nice."

"I know," Mrs Frickart said.

Patsy and I went to the computer. It stood on a wooden table with ironwork scrolling and a Singer sewing machine upside-down underneath. Another generational thing.

"You want to learn about buying things on eBay or selling?" she asked me.

"Both?"

"OK," she said. "Are you going to take notes?"

I filled a couple of notebook pages by the time Mrs Frickart interrupted us because Patsy's mother, Honey, was about due.

As I left an old yellow Ford rolled up and a woman got out. Honey looked more like her mother than her daughter but I didn't stop for introductions.

Instead I went on home. Once there I fired up my own computer. When you've been taught something, it's good to go over it all again a little while later.

So… eBay…

I looked at knickknacks around my office with brand new eyes.

8

An hour later I was about to phone LeBron but as I reached for the receiver – yes, still a landline – it tinkled.

"This is not a precedent," my daughter said by way of a greeting.

"Absolutely not," I said.

"I spoke with a woman."

"And I swear I won't expect you ever to do such a thing again."

"Shirley Downley. Her husband was in my class at the academy. She works in the office at Southeast and she's there tonight until the swing shift goes out. Call her, if you still want the information you asked me about."

She'd found me a contact... What an excellent daughter. "You're an *excellent* daughter," I said.

"But this isn't any kind of precedent. I happened to run into Chip – Downley – and he mentioned Shirley and we got to talking."

"This precedes no dent. Got it."

She gave me Shirley Downley's number.

Hah. Gotcha, my girl...

I called Southeast and Shirley was helpful and sweet. Helpful because she told me there was no pattern of burglaries in the

Beechport area in recent months. And sweet because she told me that I have an outstanding daughter. "Chip talked about her when they were in the Academy," Shirley said, "and how Sam was just one of the guys even though she was always top of the class. You must be real proud."

Is there such a thing as double-proud?

So LeBron, né Curtis, became my third phone conversation instead of my first. "What are you doing now?" I asked him.

He hesitated.

I said, "I don't want a description. I'd like to come over, but I wouldn't want to break up an alien house party if you're throwing one."

"Come over."

Night hadn't fallen but it was slipping. There's a brief time when lights are on inside houses but curtains aren't yet drawn. For a few minutes you get a glimpse into other people's lives. I've seen kisses and slaps over the years, but in this neighborhood – where eyes in those same windows keep close track of visitors – I overcame my curiosity and went straight to LeBron's.

And he opened his door before I reached his bell. Maybe he was more like his neighbors than they – or he – gave him credit for.

"No new thefts today?" I said as I went in.

"No. Do you have information about the last one?"

"As it happens, I may."

"Already?"

"Are you impressed?"

"Have you recovered my father's handprint?"

"No."

"But you know where it is?"

"No."

He frowned.

"But I may have a way to find it."

LeBron stood behind me as I sat at his computer and went to eBay. Once there I wrote "40th 'Sound of Music'" in the box labeled "keywords" and hit "search."

The screen filled with a list that promised fifty-seven anniversary sounds of music. On the left side of the list, however, I scrolled down to where I was invited to eliminate some of the fifty-seven on the basis of their "distance" from a zip code.

"What's your zip?" He gave it to me and I instructed eBay to eliminate all sounds of music more than ten miles away.

One copy of the DVD remained. It was located in Indianapolis and was offered by a seller whose "username" was "willy1". Not as many Willys in Indianapolis as Indygirls, it seemed.

Clicking on willy1 brought up willy1's page. It didn't provide an address, phone number or required size of handcuff, but there was a place to click and see what other items willy1 was offering for sale.

Seven items showed, all DVDs.

I turned to LeBron. "How many of these DVDs match items that were stolen from you yesterday?" I'd neglected to bring the list he'd given me but I guessed his answer.

We traded places and he looked. "Six of them," he said.

My guess missed by one. "Which one isn't?"

"The DVD of 'High School Musical'."

"But all of the other six?"

"Yes."

"Now look at the 'time left' on the six items that match yours." I showed him where it was.

"Six days and various numbers of hours and minutes," he said. "Are you saying those are my DVDs?"

"I'm saying that you are looking at DVDs offered for sale by a single seller who's probably within ten miles of here. If they were all listed last night for seven-day auctions then these are the times-left that we'd see. So I do believe that they're your DVDs and that your thief is trying to fence the stolen items on eBay."

"But why only six?"

"It takes some time to list an item. The thief may be busy with other things or may not have unlimited access to a computer. Tomorrow you may well see more on willy1's for-sale list."

LeBron considered. "But where is my father's handprint?"

"If I'm right, it's in willy1's house. My guess is that willy1 will offer it for sale after putting things that are easier to describe on sale first. That probably applies to the flower radio too. For DVDs you also don't need to take your own pictures. I hit the "previous screen" arrow a few times until I had the array of sounds of music from all across the country. "See how many of those pictures are the same? They're stock pictures. Using them makes it quicker to list your DVD for sale than if you take a picture yourself."

Patsy would have been proud of all the information that I had retained from my eBay lesson.

"OK," LeBron said slowly. "So how do we get the address of where my things are?"

"You can't do it on the site."

"But we must be able to find it *somehow*."

"Plan B," I said, "would be to win one of the auctions and then ask to pay by check. willy1 would have to send us the address to send the check to."

He thought about that. “You say that’s Plan B?”

“Yeah.”

“What’s Plan A?”

“You come with me now.”

I led LeBron out of his house. We turned right and went up the steps to his neighbor’s porch. I rang the bell.

I was about to ring it again when Mrs Frickart opened the door. “Why Mr Samson. And Mr Nelson. What a nice surprise.”

I turned to my client. “Mr Nelson?”

“My current name evolved after Mrs Frickart and I first met.”

“Oh I’m so sorry,” Mrs Frickart said. “You’re Mr James now.” She tapped her head. “Not working as well as it used to. Please – no offence intended.”

“And none taken.” My client surprised me by stepping forward and taking his neighbor’s hands. “You have a wonderful heart and only the best of intentions. I know that.”

“So what can I do for you fine young men? But where are my manners? Come in, come in.”

“I’m not sure you’ll think we’re such fine young men after I explain why we’re here,” I said.

9

Patsy and her mother lived in a rented house about two miles away. In the fading light I couldn't see which building had the number I was looking for, but then a door opened. A compact shape like Mrs Frickart's appeared as a shadow outline created by the light behind it.

No doubt Mrs Frickart had called Honey to tell her that we were on our way. And why.

I led as we went through the gate in a wire fence that ran around the small, boxy house. None of Beechport was fancy or fashionable in modern Indy, but this part was basic by any standards.

"One of you is Mr Samson," said the shadow.

"That's me."

"So you're Mr James, Ma's neighbor."

LeBron stepped forward and offered his hand. "I'm sorry to make your acquaintance in such awkward circumstances, Mrs…"

The tone of his voice was liquid and smooth and it won Honey over. She took his hand as she said, "It's Frickart again now. Ms."

LeBron said, "I don't know your mom well, but I do know she's proud that you've been strong enough to get out of the situation you were in."

This seemed to catch Honey by surprise. "She is?"

"Sure as sugar. Though I promise she hasn't told me any personal details."

Honey stepped back, thinking for a moment about her personal details. "Yeah, well," she said. "It's hard. But we're here now."

"And you've got your health. And your daughter. And your lovely mother nearby."

"I guess."

"May we come in?" I said before what we'd come for was replaced by a love-in.

"What? Oh. Sure." Honey led me and LeBron into a short hallway. "Patsy is getting the things she took. I am *so* embarrassed and I'll pay for the damage to your door. I don't know *what* got into her. I had no idea she was stealing, and she will be punished *very* severely."

"Please don't do that," LeBron said.

This surprised not only Honey but me.

Honey said, "She has to learn. Though Lord knows I got enough on my plate without her adding to it."

"Do you… Would you mind if I have a few words with her?" LeBron said.

"You can't possibly say anything that I haven't already told her."

"I can tell her I'm not angry and that I know she's not a *bad* girl."

"Oh." Honey looked tired. "Well. I guess. Sure, if you want to I suppose you're entitled to say whatever you want to her. Look, you go into the living room. I'll send her through."

"Thank you."

I followed LeBron. "What are you up to?" I asked quietly.

"Just what I said."

"For someone so fixed this morning on getting his missing 'handprint' back you're sounding very calm."

"What's the point of anger?"

"It's only human." He flashed a little smile. "Silly me," I said. I had no wish to see young Patsy thrashed or jailed, but still...

The small living room had three seats fanned out facing a large television set. LeBron went to the middle chair and turned it to face one next to it.

"What are you up to now?" I asked.

"You're a lot like me, you know."

"Not if you think I understand why you're playing with the furniture."

"You live in a harsh world, don't you?"

Either his craziness was leaking or he was avoiding my question. I moved to my own agenda. "Are we agreed that I've completed my work for you?"

"Of course."

"I'll make a calculation and give you some money back tomorrow."

"There's no need."

I'd been good – finding his thief so quickly – but not a thousand bucks good. "Yes there is."

"OK then." He stood back to look at the chairs. "And you can leave now, if you want to. It's not a long walk for me."

What I wanted was to see the precious handprint. "I'll stay, unless you go all feature-length."

"She's just a child," LeBron said.

And does that make her a lot like you? I asked, but not aloud because just then a reluctant Patsy appeared in the doorway. She held two shoeboxes.

She said, "I'm sorry I broke into your house and stole your stuff, all *right?* But you are a weirdo. Everybody says so."

"*Patricia!*" Honey said from behind her daughter.

"Yeah, well. Sorry. Like I said."

Quietly LeBron said, "It's not that big a deal." Then he waited.

He was waiting for Patsy to make the next move, either to speak or give him the boxes.

In the end she did both. She came into the room and said, "Really. I'm sorry. I don't know why I did it. I just took one of Memaw's knives and went over to your back door. I'm really really sorry."

But LeBron didn't take the boxes. He gestured to the chair he'd picked for her. "Sit down, please, Patsy."

Patsy glanced at her stern-faced mother, and then sat. LeBron sat facing her. "Now," he said, "show me which of my things you like best."

"What?"

"Which do you like best?"

Another glance at her mother, who shrugged. Then Patsy took the bottom box, moved some things around, and her hand came out holding a piece of limestone.

With a big smile, LeBron turned to me. "Albert, why don't you and Ms Frickart go into the kitchen and have some water or something."

I had no clue what was going on, but it didn't seem like he was about to strangle the kid. So I asked Honey if I could I have a drink of water and together we went to the kitchen.

10

"You want ice in this?" Honey asked as she ran water from the faucet into a glass.

"If it isn't too much trouble." I sat at the formica kitchen table.

"I've got ice." She took a tray from her fridge's freezing compartment. "No fans. No aircon, but I've got ice."

"It's almost never this hot at this time of year."

"I know. I grew up here." She put the ice water in front of me and dropped onto a chair across the table. "It's my fault," she said.

"The hot weather?"

"Everything but. At least it seems like it. When things hit the fan with Darnell – that's Patsy's father – I just ran for it."

"That's often the bravest thing a person can do."

She looked at me. "There was plenty of reasons, but I didn't think of Pats. I thought, She's a kid, she'll be all right. But it's been hard on her. No friends. No Blossom."

"Blossom?"

"Her horse. Well, not *her* horse, but the horse she rode and looked after. The horse she *loved.* I was never into horses myself, but Pats lives and breathes them. And that's why I helped her."

"I don't understand."

"I let her go on eBay. I set up that payment system they have, PayPal. You're supposed to be eighteen and have a bank account. She said she wanted to sell some of her things and her grandmother's things so when she found a stable she could get some lessons. I never, not for one minute, thought she'd start *stealing*."

"I don't sense that she's working up to a career as a criminal," I said.

"No, but she's hurting. And that's because of me."

"Doesn't Darnell figure?"

"We left in the night. She never got to say goodbye."

"To her father?"

"To Blossom."

I sipped from the water. "This is good."

Honey said nothing, and said it tiredly.

"May I get you some?" I said.

"What?"

"A glass of water."

"You're going to get me a glass of water in my own house?"

"Only if you want one. I'm guessing people don't do things for you very often."

After a moment she said, "Yeah, go on then."

So I did.

We sat for a while facing each other, drinking water.

"So what's your pal telling my daughter in there?"

"I have no idea."

"Well, I don't hear her crying."

"Maybe he's got his hand over her mouth."

"That's not funny."

"No. It's not."

But then we were interrupted.

Patsy came to the kitchen door, smiling broadly. "Mom, look what Mr James is going to let me keep."

LeBron appeared behind her. "Borrow," he said.

"Yeah, borrow."

"For as long as you need it."

Patsy held up the piece of limestone. It was my first look at the elusive handprint. It looked like a fossil with a leaf pattern.

11

When we were in the car and we'd gone a couple of blocks toward his home I said, "After all that you left the handprint behind?"

"She says she feels a tingle when she holds it. And it makes her feel better."

"You let her keep it because it makes her tingle and feel better?"

"Borrow it. I'll get it back. When she doesn't need it any more."

After another block I said, "Did she tell you about Blossom?"

"Her horse? Yeah."

"Honey says she wanted things to sell on eBay for riding lessons."

"Naa," LeBron said. "She stole my things to impress Willy Simberley."

"I agree, given her choice of eBay username."

"Patsy is alone in an unfamiliar and hostile world. She's an outsider, Albert. Like me. Like you. But unlike us, she isn't used to it yet. She hasn't found out the advantages."

"Which advantages would those be?"

He faced me. "You'd never trade what you are to be 'normal'. You wouldn't give up your word games, your independence."

"But I bet she would."

"Maybe."

We rode in silence for another block. It's one thing for me to say I'm abnormal but I didn't like a stranger feeling so comfortable saying it. But he wasn't wrong about my unwillingness to trade it if that meant I'd laugh along with sit-com laugh tracks and sit happily at a desk pushing paper from nine to five.

LeBron said, "I explained to Patsy about doctors."

"What about doctors?"

"Well, medical students. In their first year the students who majored in a pre-med subject do best. But long term the ones who do best *didn't* have pre-med majors. People who are different, who have a broad range of background experiences, they'll usually cope with life better in the long term than the narrow people."

"I'm glad you believe that, LeBron."

"Oh, I do, Albert. I do. And I hope Patsy can believe it too. Because what's happened to her must be something like what my father felt when he found himself abandoned in this world."

"He was abandoned?"

"Well, I don't really know. But I do know that's how Patsy feels. Alone, ignored and invisible. And if my father's handprint makes her feel better, I'm happy for her to have it for a while."

It had been a long hot day with many twists and turns. I said nothing more until we were nearly at his house. Then I asked, "Why 'LeBron James', Mr Nelson? Of all the names you could have picked..."

"He was so much better a player than everyone else from such a young age, I figure he must be one of us."

"Us?"

"Those of us who are more than just human."

There were probably defenders in the NBA who felt much the same.

"So you think you were born to be exceptional?" I said.

"I *am* exceptional."

"If you're not showing it on a basketball court, how are you showing it?"

"By helping people. And I *can* do that. The ones who aren't noticed by anybody else."

"How?"

"By noticing them."

"Stop being so detailed. Try being enigmatic."

"I can't say more than that. It's just something in me. Something that I feel."

We arrived in front of his house. Lights glowed in the houses both sides of LeBron's but I didn't feel like telling the neighbors what had happened. Memaw Frickart would find out soon enough from her beleaguered daughter. Eileen Simberley could find out if she had a brain transplant and decided to be nice to LeBron again and asked.

"Well, I hope it all works out for you," I said to him. "And get yourself a better lock on your back door."

"I'm not sure I'll have it repaired at all. Look at the good that's come out of what's happened."

He got out and went up to his porch and I drove away.

My client wouldn't be the first guy with an extra-terrestrial father to devote his life to making the world a better place. I just hoped that he'd have a longer and luckier life in the Middle West than the more famous one had in the Middle East.

GOOD INTENTIONS

It seemed like the rain would never stop. I was getting cabin fever and I wasn't even in a cabin. Had I *ever* been in a cabin? I mean, a *cabin?* I couldn't remember one. I wanted to go to a cabin. Experience Cabinness. Be thoroughly cabined. The rain seemed like it would never stop.

I was bored. There is only a certain amount that a private investigator can do constructively when he is without clients, even in a fascinating, action-packed city like Indianapolis. I'd done it and it wasn't even noon yet. We do get rains like this here but not usually in November. Or is it common in Novembers? Had the incessant rain washed my memory away?

So it was with pleasure that I thought I heard footsteps on my office stairs. Normally I'd dismiss such sounds as self-delusion – so few clients ever arrive without an appointment. And then there was the rain. I *mean...* Could I *really* be hearing footfalls among the plops of those endless raindrops?

As it turned out, I could. There was a knock at my door. Even the most savage rain doesn't do that. I dashed to respond. The last thing I wanted was for a prospective client to dissolve away.

The last thing I expected was to open the door and recognize the prospective client. My repeat clients always call, make appointments, even summon me to come to them. But then again this prospective repeat client was not a normal kinda guy.

"LeBron," I said. "Come in. Get out of the wet."

I stood back but he didn't cross the threshold. At first I thought he was being contrary, but then I saw it was hard for him to move at all. One arm hung loose at his side. His clothes were torn. He was standing askew.

"LeBron, what's wrong?"

Faintly he said something. When I leaned forward and asked him to repeat it he said, "It's Wolfgang now."

It took a while but I eventually I sat him in my Client's Chair. He groaned with each step. I sat on my desk facing him. "How badly are you hurt?"

He didn't respond.

"How badly are you hurt, Wolfgang? Should I call an ambulance?"

"We heal quickly."

I didn't like the way he held himself in my chair. I didn't like the sound of his breathing. I didn't like the sight of blood dripping onto my floor. I picked up the phone.

"No."

"Yes."

He passed out. I dialed 911.

2

St. Riley's emergency department was full, which surprised me. Ice and snow produce broken bones, but rain? What were they all here for? Near-drownings? Mold?

Whatever the answer, the emergency crew jumped Wolfgang to the head of the line. "So what happened to your friend?" asked the nurse when I followed him to a cubicle.

"I have no idea."

"What's his name?"

"Wolfgang."

"Wolfgang," the nurse said. "Interesting." She turned to him. "Wolfgang, my name is Matty. Can you hear me?"

He made a sound. I couldn't make out, like, a *word,* but Nurse Matty seemed happy with the noise itself. She turned back to me. "Has he lost consciousness since it happened?"

"He passed out when he arrived at my office, just before I called 911. Before that I don't know."

"How long ago did this happen?"

"I don't know."

"You don't know much, do you?"

"No, ma'am, I don't."

"Did you do this to him?"

"No."

"You know *that*, do you?"

"He came to where I live, dragged himself up a flight of stairs and knocked at my door. That was about…" I looked at my watch. "Fifty-seven minutes ago, when I called 911. I don't know what happened before he got to me, where it happened, when it happened or how he got to my place."

"He's… your boyfriend?"

"He's not a friend of any description. Two months ago he hired me to do a job for him. I haven't seen or spoken with him since."

"That was September?"

"Yes. I finished the job for him in a day."

"You're not a plumber by any chance?"

"No. Sorry."

She sighed. "So, why did he come to you?"

"Once you and your colleagues put Wolfgang Dumpty back together again, maybe he'll tell me."

"That's his last name? Dumpty?"

"I have no idea what his last name is. When I worked for him he called himself 'LeBron James'. If he's 'Wolfgang' now, chances are that the rest of his handle is Mozart. He has an interest in prodigies."

"What's all that supposed to mean?"

"He changes his name sometimes."

"He changes his name?" She looked from me to him and back again. "Why?"

"I'd rather he told you himself."

"Is he crazy? Is that it?"

"Personally, I think he's unusually sane. But he does have some quirks."

"You're not helping me here."

"I'm helping you as much as I can."

"Does he have medical insurance? Wait, let me guess. You don't know."

"I can probably remember his address."

"But he was rich enough to hire you for a day in November?"

"Yes."

"Are you cheap?"

"I'm fabulously expensive and worth every penny."

"A doctor will be here in a minute. I'm going to check his pockets now. They might have some ID that will help."

She checked his pockets. They were empty. Which surprised me because when he came to my office in September he was carrying a lot of cash. So maybe he'd been robbed.

"Go tell them what you can at the desk," she said.

"And will you let me know when you find out what's wrong with him?"

"You're waiting around?"

"Yeah."

"Even though you're not a friend?"

"I give good customer aftercare."

She made a face at me.

I left to deliver a second batch of "I don't know"s at the reception desk.

3

I expected to be left to my own devices in the waiting room for a long time but Nurse Matty came to get me less than a quarter of an hour after I picked a seat.

"You *are* still here."

"Didn't you expect me to be?"

"Not after we found your friend – no, your non-friend – has stab wounds."

"That's not nice."

"No it's not."

"And you thought I was the stabber and had made a run for it."

"Look, can you come with me and go through what you know with our head of security?"

"While you wait for the cops to come and have me go through what I know with them?"

"Or hunt you down like a stray dog if you don't stay. Your call," she said with a bit of a smile.

"Why don't you tell me something about Wolfgang's prognosis."

"The doctor found two wounds in his belly before I came to look for you. Neither looked deep or in a vital place but they'll take him up to an operating theater in a few minutes to make sure."

"And has he said anything about what happened or who did it?"

"He's been mumbling things. Maybe an old friend like you will be able to understand him better than I can."

I followed Matty into the treatment labyrinth. I wasn't sure what to tell the security people – or the cops. When I knew him, Wolfgang's fickleness about names wasn't his main peculiarity. That honor fell to his insistence that his father was an extra-terrestrial.

But with me he behaved rationally and paid cash. By no means all the terrestrials I deal with do either.

The security guy was a woman who was taller, younger and arguably more muscular than I am. She waited for me at the foot of Wolfgang's bed but as I was about to introduce myself, the patient spotted me and tried to sit up.

He said, "Albert."

It was quiet but clear enough enough for Nurse Matty to ask, "Is that you?"

I nodded and went closer to his head.

"Four of them," he whispered.

"Who were they?"

What he'd already said seemed to have left him exhausted. But then he made one last effort and said what sounded like, "Terrorists…"

4

Once the magic "t" word was passed on to the police two officers in uniform soon homed in on me like I was the door to their future careers. By then Wolfgang was in surgery.

I followed the cops to a visitors' room but it didn't take me long to repeat my collection of "I don't know"s. However it was enough for Nurse Matty to stick her head in with an update. "Sorry to bother you, officers," she said, "but the surgeon upstairs believes that the two abdominal wounds were done with different knives."

The uniforms looked at each other. I said, "How do you tell something like that?"

"Think about an ordinary knife," she said. "One side sharp, one side blunt."

"OK."

"And think about it being pressed through skin. Once the point goes in, one side of the wound is cut by the sharp edge but the other is just rubbed by the blunt one. Maybe torn open a little, but not cut. The result is that the two ends of the wound look completely different under magnification."

"Sounds reasonable," I said.

"Apparently one of the blades that cut him had *two* sharp edges, whereas the other had only one. That's what he says. He also says that he can't be completely certain without doing an autopsy."

I leaned forward.

"But he doesn't think it'll come to that," she said. "Oh. And they found another cut. On his back. Not as deep. He didn't say if he thinks it was done by one of the original two knives." She left.

"She says there were three wounds, not two?" the smaller of the two cops asked.

I nodded. Poor ol' Wolfgang.

The smaller cop crossed something out in his notebook and wrote a correction.

The larger cop just said, "What's he expect?" He was a big guy who looked the age and size of a high school lineman.

"What do you mean?" his colleague asked.

"He said it was terrorists," the lineman said. "If he's going to mess with terrorists..." He looked from his colleague to me, looking for support.

I said, "If someone is attacked by terrorists, the *victim* is responsible?" I shook my head. "You're saying the people who died on 9/11 were *messing* with terrorists?"

"I just said..." the lineman began. But he stopped.

His colleague smiled and shook his head slowly.

I said nothing more. And at least they had treated me as a witness rather than a suspect, probably because Nurse Matty had stressed that I stayed around after Wolfgang came in.

But with the patient in surgery and the uniforms unable to think of more questions for me not to know the answers to, I began to consider leaving. However then a southside detective, Imberlain, showed up. So I got to do it all again.

By which time Matty had a further update. The surgeons had found a fourth cut. They were now putting Wolfgang's spleen and liver back together. So I decided to leave, at least for the time being.

I'd followed the ambulance in my car, so I had wheels. But instead of using them to go back home, I went to Wolfgang's house.

He had showed up at my office about eleven-thirty. Now it was nearly four, and still raining. I didn't know when he'd been attacked by the "terrorists" but he'd been away from home for many hours.

Though when I got there it didn't seem like the house was empty. Through the rain I could see some lights on inside. But not behind curtained windows. I could see them through the wide-open door.

I parked and went to the porch. It was then that I discovered the door wasn't wide open after all. It had been pulled off its hinges.

5

I had no idea what Wolfgang had been doing in the two months since I'd last seen him. Then he was hale and hearty – not a single stab wound. He had talked optimistically about his future, wanting to create a project to help the people he described as society's "invisibles".

And when I'd last visited his house, the interior was immaculate. Wolfgang – though then he was LeBron – had converted the conventional interior into a large space. He'd done all the work himself, having trained as a carpenter. As well he'd painted pictures and designs on the walls. There wasn't much furniture when I'd been there, just what a half-alien gentleman would use when living on his own.

But now, coming through the open doorway, I saw pieces of furniture everywhere. Most seemed once to have come from beds, and there were also mattresses ripped open.

This was clearly a matter for the police, though none were on the scene.

Which left me with a decision to make. I ought to call Imberlain, who'd given me his card. But my impulse was to call my daughter. She was a cop just off her probationary year. Sam didn't work southeast but Wolfgang's house wasn't far from the southwest sector where she did work. And she, at least, was used to me. She wouldn't ask me endless questions about why I'd gone to Wolfgang's house instead of going home.

"Why did you call me, Daddy?"

"You're a cop. This is a police matter."

"Call 911."

"It isn't an emergency. The house isn't on fire. The front door's been ripped off its hinges. The owner's in hospital with four stab wounds. There are a few lights on but I don't know if anyone's inside. I didn't want to go in without somebody knowing where I am and what I'm doing."

"So naturally you called me."

"My daughter, the cop. Naturally." I said, "I'm not asking you to drop whatever you're doing and rush out here, but would you stay on the phone while I go in?"

"You shouldn't go in. It's a crime scene. You should call the police."

"I did call the police. And what if someone's in there, and injured?"

"Call 327 3811. That's the number for non-emergencies."

"I'm going in." I was already inside the front door, but dwelling on details would be pedantic.

"Call the number, Daddy."

"Just hang on while I look around."

"Daddy!"

Slowly I walked into the middle of the open room. It was chaos. A large television set had been tipped off its mounting. DVDs were scattered over a whole corner. In the kitchen area large pans were on the floor. More and larger pans than I would have thought a man living alone would have. Mind you, there were pieces from a lot of beds – I counted what looked like half a dozen without trying. How many people were sleeping here? Had Wolfgang set up an open-plan B&B?

"Daddy?"

"I'm here, honey. Just hang on."

"I'm hanging up."

"Please don't do that."

Given the beds, I was interested in what I didn't see. Which was evidence of people – their bags, their clothes… Such things might be underneath the wreckage, but I saw nothing on top.

I made my way to the back door. That was still on its hinges but it swung loose in the bits of breeze that passed through the house.

I didn't get it.

"Daddy, I'm hanging up."

I was about to say OK and that she should get back to whatever or whomever she was doing when I heard a whimper.

"Hang on. I hear something. Or someone."

"Who?"

"I'm looking."

I followed the sound. I found its source in the bathroom. It was a child. "It's a little boy."

The kid looked up sharply. He had tear-stained eyes. "I'm a girl," he said.

"I mean a little girl."

"How old?" Sam asked.

"About… seven."

"I'm ten."

"I mean ten. She's about ten. And her name is Jane."

"Nicole," the girl said.

"I mean Nicole. And she's resting in the bathroom because she just broke all the furniture here and destroyed the place."

"I'm hiding," Nicole said. "I was scared."

6

Sam arrived about half an hour later. She wasn't wearing her uniform.

"Thanks for coming," I said. "I didn't know what to do."

"I hope you didn't disturb anything."

"I had to think of Nicole." Nicole looked up from a chair she was using as a table in the kitchen area. "She was hungry."

"Thirsty," Nicole said.

"And thirsty. I made her a glass of water."

"You don't *make* water," Nicole said.

"And I *made* her cinnamon toast." I stuck my tongue out at the child. She laughed. I turned to Sam. "Like I used to make for you."

"Is that your wife?"

"My daughter."

"Is that *really* your daughter?" Nicole asked.

"My lovely daughter, of whom I am double-proud."

"Why double?"

"Proud of her as an outstanding police person and proud of her as a wonderful human being who has come through a lot of difficulties in her life."

Nicole frowned. "She's police?"

"Sure as shootin'."

Sam drew me aside. "What do you know about her?" I shook my head. "Or about what happened?" I shrugged.

"I waited for you before asking questions," I said.

Sam looked at her watch.

"Do you have to be somewhere?"

"I called this in on my way. Some uniforms should be here soon." She knelt beside Nicole's "table." "I'm Sam," she said.

"That's a *boy's* name."

"My father wanted a boy. He didn't realize that girls are better."

That pleased the child, who acknowledged it by taking a giant mouthful of the toast, as if no mere boy could eat so much at one time. She choked a little but got it down.

Sam said, "I need you to tell me what happened here, Nicole."

"Men came and wanted money. Wolfgang wouldn't give it to them so they looked everywhere for it. Then they took him away."

"Wolfgang?" Sam asked.

"He owns the house," I said.

"The men broke everything," Nicole said. "It wasn't me."

"Who else was here?"

"Two of the mothers." Nicole thought. "Tara and… I can't remember her name."

"They were staying here?" Sam asked.

"We all stay here."

"Why is that?"

"Our husbands and boyfriends aren't good ones. They hit us." Her face wrinkled. "Not me. But Mom. Harvey does that."

"Is Harvey your dad?"

"No." Her frown suggested that the less she had to do with Harvey the happier she'd be.

"How many women are staying here?" Sam asked.

Nicole counted on her fingers. "Seven."

"And children?"

"Only me and a couple of babies."

"Where are they all now?" Sam asked.

"Tara and the other one ran away when the men came. Two others… Janine and Stephanie… They came back later but they left. I think it was because their kids were about to get out of school." She thought. "That's Harry after the prince of England cause he's got red hair, and Chloe."

"They go to school?" Sam said. "I thought you said only babies stayed here."

"Harry's six and Chloe is seven. They're *such* babies."

"And," Sam said, "where is *your* mother, Nicole?"

After toughing it out for a moment, Nicole's face puckered up. She began to cry. "I don't know. She left this morning and said I should wait here."

"And you haven't seen her or heard from her?"

"I *told* her I should have my own phone."

"Why aren't you at school?"

"The one I go to is too far away. Mom said we'd get a new one soon."

"She wasn't here when the men came?"

"No."

"Do you know where she went? To work, maybe?"

"She used to work at Dennys but then Harvey found her. I don't know if she found another job yet." Another pucker. "But she always comes back at night. I wait here for her." She looked up at Sam. "Do you think Harvey found her again?"

"I don't know," Sam said quietly, "but I'll try to find out. So Harvey wasn't one of the men who took Wolfgang away?"

"I don't know. They had masks on."

"What kind of masks?"

"All over their faces, with holes for the eyes."

"Did you recognize any of the men?"

She shook her head.

I said, "Do you know Harvey's last name?"

"Peterson, I think."

"Does Harvey know you and your mother live here now?"

"I don't think so. But we've only been here…" She thought. "Three nights. But even if Harvey comes Wolfgang promised he won't get in."

"How does he make sure of that?"

"He locks the door and he's the only one who answers it." The face puckered again. "But when the men came, they just pushed him out of the way. Wolfgang shouted for everyone to run and he jumped on one of the men, on his back."

"You must have been scared, Nicole," I said.

She nodded.

"But you didn't leave with the other women?"

"Mom said to wait here."

There was noise at the front of the house. We turned to look and saw two cops coming in through the aforementioned – but empty – doorway.

Sam put her arm around Nicole and took control.

I took flight.

7

I headed back to the hospital. The answers to most of my questions were knocking around somewhere in Wolfgang's head. Wolfgang, the half-alien formerly known as LeBron James, Wolfgang, the half-alien born in Santa Claus, Indiana, under the name of Curtis Nelson.

I did know *some* things.

As I drove I thought about what Nicole had told us and I wondered what kind of place Wolfgang was running. The Wolfgang I'd known didn't seem a first choice candidate for defender against angry terrorists, or boyfriends. He wasn't big – just a medium kind of guy. And when I knew him he didn't even have secure locks on his doors.

However at that time he'd lived alone. Now he lived with seven women and three children. Maybe other things had changed too.

Once inside the hospital I was waylaid in the crowded waiting room. The rain hadn't stopped and people continued to flood into Emergency. However I said magic words. I asked for Nurse Matty by name. Moments later she appeared before me.

"You're back," she said.

"Your powers of observation continue to dazzle."

"I thought this Wolfgang guy wasn't a friend."

"He's not. However I've just been to his house where the cops are sifting through the wreckage of all the furniture."

She leaned forward with her eyes wide open. "*Wreckage?*"

"There was also a ten-year-old girl hiding there who doesn't know where her mother is."

"This is Wolfgang's… girlfriend?"

"Unlikely, but he's the only person I can think of who might have an idea what's up with mom. And if he's anywhere close to conversation-enabled, I need to see him."

Nurse Matty tilted her head. "So, does that make you a cop?"

"No. But my daughter is."

She blinked a couple of time. "Does *anything* you say make sense?"

"I've been asked that before."

"I'm going to take you to see him anyway."

"Thank you."

"But you've got to promise not to stab him. We've sewn him up enough for one day. We found a fourth cut – in his shoulder from the back. Did I tell you that before?"

"Not where it was."

She turned and we walked. "He's in a recovery room."

"Not intensive care then?"

"He should be fine. Only one of the abdominal wounds was deep. There were perforations in his liver and pancreas, but not big ones. The shoulder will give him trouble for a long time, but your Wolfgang is a very lucky boy."

"I wonder if he sees it that way yet." After a couple of turns, I said, "Were the four wounds all with different knives? Could they tell?"

"I don't know."

"They didn't find he has two hearts by any chance, did they?"

She stopped abruptly and looked at me. "What is *that* supposed to mean?"

"Don't mind me."

"That he loves you but he loves somebody else too?"

"I know nothing whatever about this love life, if any."

"I don't know if he's going to make much sense yet," she said, "so you should be a perfect pair."

"This whole situation doesn't make any sense," I said.

"No?"

"Like, why did he come to *me*?"

Outside some drawn curtains, Matty said, "Remember, people take different lengths of time to come around after a general anesthetic." She opened a gap in the curtains and I went in.

8

Wolfgang was not looking his best. The side of his head was bandaged – though I hadn't heard about a head injury – and there were enough drips and tubes and machines to make Baron Münchhausen envious.

But he responded to the noise of my arrival and he moved to sit up while I pulled a chair close. "Mr Albert Samson," he said. "Greetings."

"Mr Wolfgang… would that be Mozart?"

"It would." Not too spaced-out to smile.

"How's it going?"

"I've felt better. But we heal quickly."

"You told me that before. Do you remember?"

He thought. He didn't remember.

"Have you healed enough to answer some questions?"

"I'll try."

"Your house is a wreck."

"That's not a question."

"Why are seven women and three children living with you?"

"Not *living*."

"They have – had – beds. They come home to your place after they finish work. What do *you* call it?"

"Visiting."

"Silly me."

"It wasn't my plan."

"Women, some with children, just started appearing at your door?"

"It began with one. I was walking around and I found this woman leaning against a fence. She'd been beaten up."

"You *found* her?"

"About two miles from my house – in fact a little closer to yours than mine."

"So you dialed 911?"

"She didn't want me to do that."

"Why not?"

"Do you know anything about the psychology of battered women?"

"Do you?"

"I've been reading up on it. Anyhow, I brought her home. I got her a bed. The idea was that she could stay for a few days, until she felt better."

"When was this?"

"Second week in October."

"And is she still visiting you?"

"Well, yes."

"And she happened to have some buddies who also got beaten up?"

"I guess. Or some kind of word started spreading around. Women, and children…"

"But there are shelters in the city, Wolfgang. Organized places with much better facilities than just having beds scattered around an open space, all sharing one bathroom."

"And one kitchen… I know. Dayspring, the Julian Center… I have a list and I tell them. And some have gone to them. But a lot don't want to."

"They all stayed on?"

"A lot have gone back to where they came from." He shook his head sadly.

I said, "Back in September you talked about doing something for 'invisible' people."

"This wasn't what I meant. I want to do something to *help* people with problems. But now all I do is squeeze more beds in and try to keep them from squabbling. I hate raised voices."

He paused. I just waited. Any group of people crowded in together isn't going to last as happy families. The Big Brother television shows made fortunes on that principle.

Wolfgang said, "I don't want my house to be a refuge for anyone but me. And I'm sure the neighbors don't like it. But if people are in trouble, how can I say no to them?"

"Practice makes perfect," I said.

"But the best part…" He smiled with some life in his eyes.

"What?"

"Sometimes they hold my father's handprint and they say it makes them feel *better*."

I knew all about the "handprint", supposedly left by his extra-terrestrial father. In the real world it was a piece of limestone with some grooves in it that looked like the fossilized veins of a leaf. Last I'd heard it was out on loan to a troubled girl who was nearly fourteen. But it was always going to be returned when she didn't need it anymore.

"They feel 'better'?"

"It calms them. They say it makes them more positive about life and the future. Sometimes we sit in a circle and pass it around."

"The psychological equivalent of homeopathy?"

"They tell me they feel something. I feel something. Maybe if you'd hold it you'd feel something too."

"I guarantee I'd feel whatever a guy giving me a safe place to sleep and food to eat wanted me to feel."

He tilted his head with a world-weary smile.

I said, "I didn't see the stone in the wreckage."

"It wasn't out. I keep it in a safe place."

"So the police in your house won't be in danger of feeling better by stumbling across it?"

"Police?"

"You were cut up. Your house is a wreck. What do you expect?"

"I guess."

"Wolfgang, what *happened*? You were stabbed four times, maybe with as many as four different knives. Did everyone want a piece? Like when the Brutus gang hit Julius Caesar?"

"They weren't trying to kill me. They were trying to get me to tell them where I keep my money."

"What *happened*?"

"Four men came to the door wearing masks. I wouldn't let them in, but they broke the door down and grabbed me and said they wanted money."

"So it was money rather than being connected to the women you were sheltering?"

"Yes and no." He smiled.

"Will I get a straight answer if I whack that bandaged shoulder with a saline drip bag?"

He didn't like the sound of that.

"When I asked you before, you said it was terrorists."

He shook his head.

"It's what you told me," I said.

"They had terrorists' *masks*."

"I only heard 'terrorists'. So you were talking about their masks, not them?"

He nodded.

"Because I didn't hear the apostrophe, the city of Indianapolis is on a rainbow alert."

"They just wanted money. For some reason they thought I keep enough money around the place to be worth robbing me."

"Do you keep a lot of money around?"

"You never know when you're going to need cash. Especially with a lot of mouths to feed."

"And beds to buy." He nodded. "How many women have stayed in your house since October?"

"Maybe twenty. Twenty-five."

"Do you keep records?"

"Of what?"

"Well, like their full names and Social Security numbers."

"I'm extra-terrestrial, not anal."

"And do you get a lot of men coming to the door?"

"A few. Husbands and boyfriends. A violent girlfriend once too. Not often."

"So what happened when the four guys in terrorists' masks demanded your money?"

"I wouldn't give it to them."

"Why not?"

He smiled. "Guess?"

I stood up and threatened his shoulder. But as he winced I put it together. "You keep your money in the same place as the handprint?"

"Yes." A smile.

"So you got yourself cut to pieces because you were protecting that damned chunk of rock."

"Whoever told them about the money might have told them how much the handprint means to me. I couldn't bear to lose it again."

So he'd rather die. I guess I just don't understand extra-terrestrials… "They wanted money. You wouldn't give it to them. What happened then?"

"They showed me the knives but when I still wouldn't do it the leader cut me – not deep, but enough to draw blood. There were a couple of women in the house and that set them off screaming and they ran. The men started cutting up mattresses and couches and everything they could see that might have money in it. But eventually the leader said they should take me with them, so they bundled me into a car."

"Right there, in front of your house?"

"Yes."

"What kind of car was it?"

"Quite large. Quite old. Light green or maybe light blue."

Not a description to conjure up a car with, but the kind of neighborhood Wolfgang lived in would probably provide the police plenty of witnesses.

"Where did they take you?"

"They just drove around."

"And continued to cut you in the car?"

"They didn't know what else to do. But then..."

"What?"

"They gave up. The shoulder was bleeding so much the driver complained about the car upholstery and how they'd never be able to clean the DNA off it. He said he didn't want to burn his car and they started arguing with each other."

"Obviously a gang of master criminals."

"So they dumped me out, behind the Murphy building and I recognized it."

The old Murphy five and dime was across Virginia Avenue from my office. That was one question answered.

"So you came to me," I said.

"I didn't have a phone. They took the stuff in my pockets."

"What was in them?"

"The usual things. Keys, wallet, phone."

"Much money?"

"A couple of hundred."

"The police are going to want to hear in detail what these guys said, anything you can remember about the car, and maybe names of the women staying with you."

"You don't want those things?"

"Are you hiring me?"

"Well, no. But I thought…"

"The cops probably won't have much trouble tracking down your assailants. And when they find them they'll have the advantage of the power of arrest."

"I see."

Which made me wonder something. "Wolfgang, could the guys who attacked you have been neighbors of yours?"

"Neighbors?" A deep frown.

"From families who don't like the idea of your opening your house to waifs and strays."

"Well…" He thought about it. "I don't know *who* they were."

"Did they say anything about your moving somewhere else, say?"

He shook his head. "It seemed to be all about the money. I've had some problems with my neighbors but I can't imagine…"

"OK," I said. Though there seemed to be quite a lot he couldn't imagine, at one time or another. Why people didn't just accept him as an extra-terrestrial, for instance. "I do want something else."

"What?"

"I found a little girl in your house. She was hiding and must have been there for hours."

"Who?"

"Nicole? She's ten."

He nodded. "Elaine's little girl."

"Elaine hasn't come back."

"That's surprising. She's a very attentive mother."

"Nicole was surprised too…"

9

I had no reason to think that Elaine was in the kind of trouble that would lead her to court. But a woman desperate enough to run with her child from a boyfriend was not going to leave that kid unattended if she could help it.

The police would get onto it eventually, no doubt. But as long as they could drop the kid into the Welfare system they'd focus first on the wreckage and the stabbings. That's how police prioritize. Even those related to me by blood. Unless given a little guidance.

I had no specific reason to connect Elaine's absence to the attack on Wolfgang, but I don't believe in coincidence much more than I believe in extra-terrestrials. One way or another there was a connection. And the only person I knew who could tell me more about Elaine was Nicole.

I called Sam.

"Where are you, Daddy?" she asked.

"Funny thing. I was about to ask you the same question."

"A detective named Saul Imberlain wants to talk to you."

"I already talked to him, at the hospital."

"He wants to talk to you again, so I gave him your address and phone number."

"I haven't been home. But look, love, I need to talk some more with the little girl, Nicole. Do you know where she is?"

"She's still here."

"Wolfgang's house?"

"I'm waiting with her till someone from the Department of Child Services shows up. Which won't be long."

"So her mother hasn't appeared?"

"No."

"Just don't let Nicole go anywhere before I get there, OK?"

"Why not?" I could hear her not saying she wasn't on duty.

"Because I'm trying to find her mother and if I can do that it'll save the poor kid some grief."

After a moment Sam said, "OK."

What a good girl.

10

Wolfgang's house looked lit up like a roaring fire now that the light was fading. The cops seemed to have turned on every light in the place.

Which is not to say there weren't a few lights aglow elsewhere along the street. Dim ones, with just enough illumination for neighbors to find their cigarettes and lemonade without making a mess as they watched the goings-on from behind their curtains. The neighbors were curious, but were they hostile?

A carpenter was at work on a temporary repair to the front door as I went in. Sam sat with Nicole in the kitchen area. A tall guy with a brown and gray beard stood behind them. Sam got up when she saw me. The tall guy pulled out a notebook.

Sam said, "This is Whitney Moser of DCS. Department of Child Services."

Moser offered a hand.

I shook it. I like to give people the benefit of the doubt.

Sam said, "Mr Moser is going to take Nicole to where she can sleep tonight."

"I need to ask her a few questions," I said.

"And she needs to get settled for the night so she can get some sleep," Moser said. "You can't treat a child the way you might treat an adult."

I crouched to be on a level with Nicole. Admittedly, she looked sleepy. It wasn't all that late, but she'd had a shocking day. "Hi," I said.

"Hi."

"Which would you rather do, Nicole?" I asked. "Get some sleep or help me find your mother?"

"Daddy!" Sam said as Moser said, "Honestly, Mr Samson."

"Help find Mom," Nicole said. She was plenty awake now.

"I need you to tell me some things that no one but you knows."

"OK."

"Do you know the address where you and your mom lived with Harvey?"

"Who's Harvey?" I heard Moser whisper to Sam.

Nicole said, "3117 Hincot Street."

"Good girl. And does your mom have any friends around there?"

"Laurie across the street."

"Right across the street?"

She nodded. "With the orange door. Mom wanted one but Harvey said no."

"Shall I get you an orange door for Christmas?"

She nodded, vigorously considering how tired she was.

"What school did you go to before you and your mom moved here?"

"Ninety-three."

"Did you like it there?"

Nod.

"I bet they liked you there too."

A little shrug. Then a nod.

"What's your mom's name?"

"Elaine."

"Elaine what?"

"Warren."

"And are she and Harvey married or is he your mom's boyfriend?"

"No."

"No?"

"He *was* her boyfriend. We don't put up with him anymore."

"And does your mom have any brothers or sisters that you know about?"

"Bobby. But he died."

"Oh, I'm sorry to hear that."

"He did magic. He found an egg in my ear."

I took a close look at one of her ears. "Yeah, I'd say there was room for an egg in there."

She smiled as she rubbed the ear in question.

I said, "And how about your mom's parents. Do you know them?"

A nod.

"Where do they live?"

"Crawfordsville."

"Are their names Mr and Mrs Warren?"

A nod, but then uncertainty. "I guess."

"Do you know their first names?"

"She's Lily. He's… Um. Oh, he's Wayne."

"And do you like them?"

A nod.

"My grandmother used to make pies, just for me," I said. "Does Lily do that for you?"

Shake of the head.

"Well, I'll tell her to get her act together," I said.

"Yeah!" Nicole said. Then she yawned.

I said, "I'm going to let you go sleep now."

Nicole looked from me to Moser and back to me. "I want to stay here, in case Mom comes home."

"I'll see what we can arrange." I gestured to Sam to take over distracting the little girl.

I led the social worker a few feet away. "Look," I said, "I know you want to get this all settled."

"I want what's best for Nicole," Moser said.

"If I can find her mother in a reasonable amount of time, that would be best, wouldn't it?"

"As long as she's able to provide a safe environment."

"Can you hang on here for a while?"

"Do you know where Elaine Warren is?"

I was tempted to say yes just to get the guy to agree but I saw Nicole paying attention to us. "Not for sure, but I have an idea. And I'll give finding her a damn good try. Plus, you've seen that Nicole doesn't want to leave. I'd appreciate it if you'll give me some time."

Moser looked at his watch.

I said, "Think about all the paperwork you'll save if I'm successful."

Moser turned out to be one of the good ones.

11

Whitney Moser began to gather bits of bed and bedding to make Nicole a place to sleep and I took Sam to the front porch. "He's going to stay here with Nicole while I can have a crack at finding Elaine."

"Where is she?" Sam said.

"I have no idea."

"Great."

"But I might know someone who does."

"I want to help, if I can, Daddy."

"Officially or as a caring human being?"

"Can you stop being you for a moment and just tell me what you have in mind?"

I had a moment in which I visualized Wolfgang the extra-terrestrial in his hospital bed, bandaged and receiving drips. My feeling of isolation from the world I inhabit can be as self-created as his. "Sorry. I'm going to try to become a better person."

"Perhaps you can postpone that too," she said, looking at her watch.

"I want to start by looking at 3117 Hincot Street. If I can find it."

"Want to follow me and my GPS?"

Hincot was a short, dead end street behind an old shopping center a couple of miles south of the city's center. It didn't appear to be a bad neighborhood, but then again it didn't *appear* much at all. The GPS had brought us to a dark stretch between two streetlights that didn't work. Or that had been shot out. I've never owned a gun in all my years as a PI but for a moment I was glad Sam-the-cop was packing.

However the only trouble we encountered was not being able to see the house numbers without our flashlights, what with the darkness and the rain.

But we found 3117, which turned out to be the top half of a duplex. Both halves were dark.

"What do you think?" Sam asked.

"I'm going to walk around back in case Harvey's sitting in his kitchen drinking himself silly by candlelight. You could make a note of the license plate numbers of the cars parked nearby along the street."

"You think one of them is Harvey's?"

There were only a few cars on the street, none parked in front of the duplex so the chances weren't good that they were relevant. But who knew?

My squishy stroll around the property did not reveal Harvey lit up round back. Or any evidence of occupation at all. There were also no cars on the alley pull-in space behind the house. Maybe everyone was out partying.

But when I returned to the front Sam's was not the only umbrella over the sidewalk. She was talking with a woman.

Sam said, "Daddy, this is Laurie. She lives—"

"Across the street and has an orange door." I stepped forward with a hand extended. "Nicole told us about you. Once we checked to see whether Harvey was at home we were going to come over and see you."

Laurie's hand was soft and warm, both pleasant qualities to experience when you're standing under an umbrella on a cold, rainy night.

"Are you a cop too?" Laurie asked.

Sam said, "Laurie came over because she thought we looked like we were police."

"I leave the weighty burden of badge-carrying to the youngsters," I said.

"I thought maybe you were here because you'd arrested Harvey and wanted to check out his house, that kind of thing," Laurie said.

"Laurie," I said, "why do you think Harvey's done something to be arrested for?"

"Can you see my face?" she asked, and turned her head.

Sam lit Laurie's face with her flashlight, revealing puffy bruising around her left ear and cuts that looked like scratches on her neck.

"Are you saying Harvey did that?" I asked.

"He certainly did."

"Why?"

"He thought I knew where Elaine was, that I was holding out on him."

"When was this?"

"This morning."

"And did you report the assault to the police?"

She hesitated, maybe working out that her answer could be checked. "No."

"Why not?"

"He said it would be my word against his and that if I told the police he and his friends would come back and *really* hurt me."

Sam said, "And do you know where Elaine is?"

Laurie hesitated over this too.

I said, "Elaine's with you, isn't she?"

"What?" both women said.

"Elaine is in your house right now," I said. "That's why you couldn't to do anything that might result in Harvey coming back and coming in."

Elaine Warren met us just inside the orange door. "Has Harvey been arrested?" she asked Laurie. "They're cops, right? He's been arrested, right?" She looked from me to Sam and back to Laurie. None of us spoke. "What? What?"

"The girl's a cop," Laurie said. "And, no, Harvey hasn't been arrested."

"Why *not?*" Elaine was clearly agitated.

Laurie put her arms around her friend and made a face at us to say we shouldn't upset her more.

I wasn't that worried about upsetting her, but I said, "That's a lovely daughter you have, Elaine."

"What?" She looked up and pulled away from Laurie's support.

"Nicole. Bright, funny. A real credit to you."

"Is she all right?"

"She's fine. We've left her with a guy from Child Services."

"Child Services?" New panic. "But Wolfgang said he'd look after her," Elaine said.

"Wolfgang is in the hospital, Mrs Warren," Sam said. "He was attacked by four men and stabbed several times."

"No," Elaine said, with disbelief. "*No!*" she cried.

I said, "So the Child Services guy is waiting with Nicole at Wolfgang's. They both hope you'll come back tonight to pick her up."

"How can I do that?" Elaine was more agitated than ever. "Where could we go? If Harvey sees me, I'm a dead woman."

"You think he's still looking for you?" Sam said.

"Unless you people lock him away."

"Elaine," I said, "when we came in, why did you ask if Harvey'd been arrested?"

"Because he's dangerous, and evil. Look what he did to Laurie."

"But the police didn't know what he did to Laurie."

Elaine looked from me to Sam to Laurie. "I just thought..."

"What?"

"Oh, I don't know. I don't *know.* I need to get Nicole. But I *can't.* If he sees me..."

"You think he'll be waiting for you outside Wolfgang's?"

She thought. "He could be. He probably is. Oh God!"

"Well, suppose we bring Nicole here for the time being."

Sam looked at me uncertainly.

"Would you?" Elaine said. She sounded more hopeful than at any previous time in the conversation. "Will you? Please!"

12

As soon as Laurie's orange door closed behind us, Sam said, "Whitney Moser's not going to let us bring Nicole here. Not with a dangerous guy on the loose who's already threatened to come back to Laurie's."

"No?"

"I wouldn't."

I said nothing.

"Daddy?"

"Yes, dear?"

"What are you up to?"

"Tell me, if you were Harvey and you were looking for Elaine, where would you wait for her?"

Sam considered. "Wolfgang's maybe."

"Once you've seen the cop cars there? Given that Elaine all but told us that he was one of the gang that stabbed Wolfgang."

"She did?"

"She expected him to be *arrested*, honey. Even Wolfgang the extra-terrestrial doesn't claim to read minds and if he can't, then the police sure can't. Arrested for what, since Laurie didn't report him?"

"If he *was* part of that," Sam said, "then he wouldn't hang around while the cop cars were there."

"So what would be your second choice as a place to wait for Elaine?"

"Well," Sam said, "here, I guess. If he thinks Laurie is helping her."

"And tell me, did you get a chance to look at the cars parked along the street?"

"Yes. But I haven't called them in."

I said, "Were the windows of any of the cars fogged up with condensation?"

13

Sam and I got in our cars and drove away.

Around the corner and then another block for luck. Sam called for a couple of squad cars to join her, stressing that they must do it quietly and must avoid Hincot Street.

The rain might have brought a lot of people out to the ER but it seemed to have kept most of Indy's malfeasors at home. Patrolling cops were bored. The call for two cars brought five.

Under Sam's guidance a couple of them drove up the alley behind 3117 with their lights out and using handbrakes to keep their brake lights from giving the game away. Once they were in place at the end of the street, Sam and the other patrol cars filled the street from its open end.

I walked back to the corner to watch. While I waited for Sam to give the go, a gust of wind blew my umbrella inside out. Then another gust righted it, but left me with a droopy corner – the umbrella would never be the same again. Was it a metaphor for life? We survive our trials but we're never quite the same?

Suddenly the six cars leapt into action, lighting the street with head, spot and blue-revolving lights. Moments later Harvey's car was surrounded with guns brandished by cops in raincoats. I saw his car's door open a crack. The first thing out was his hands held high and in plain sight. Once he was standing by the car, even from a distance he looked like he didn't know what had hit him.

I wondered if Harvey figured that his windows being steamed up would make him inconspicuous because no one could see him in the car. Wrong. His being the only car on the street with opaque windows made it more conspicuous, not less. Poor Harvey. Not one of nature's deep thinkers, at a guess.

Elaine didn't *think* Harvey had a gun, but in Indiana you can never be sure. Hence the aggressive posture of the bored police officers. As it turned out, he was as unarmed as he was unaware. They didn't even find his knife.

While the assembled representatives of law enforcement secured him ready for transfer downtown, I crossed and went back to Laurie's orange door, my umbrella's new flap flapping in the wind.

14

Whitney Moser was sitting on a kitchen chair, concentrating on his phone. Either he was dealing with weighty matters of child protection or he was playing on one of his game apps. Nicole was asleep at his feet, curled up on a nest of mattress leftovers.

Elaine followed me into the house but as soon as she saw Nicole she rushed to her and took her in her arms.

"Mom?" Nicole said as she rubbed her eyes and opened them.

It would have broken my heart if she'd woken up like that for anybody else.

Moser and I stepped away and I explained that the abusive boyfriend was now in custody, that Elaine and Nicole could go safely to the duplex where they'd been living or stay with a friend across the street.

"That's just as well," Moser said, "because I couldn't allow them to stay on here."

I thought he meant because of the lack of whole beds but that wasn't it.

"The guy who owns this place," Moser said, "what's his name?"

"Wolfgang. I'm not sure what his full name is." By now he might have changed it again, to that of someone else whose precociousness he suspected of identifying a fellow extra-terrestrial.

"Well, I've checked the address and he doesn't have any of the permits he needs to run a refuge, *especially* one with children."

"I don't think Wolfgang intended this place to become anything formal. He just took in people who asked him for help."

"Well, he'll have to learn to say no," Moser said, "unless he goes through the authorization procedure. But even if he gets personal clearance, his chances of being approved for one big open plan room..."

"He means well," I said. "I can't say more than that."

Moser gave me a card. "Have him get in touch with me if he wants to talk about his options."

I took the card.

But my lack of enthusiasm for bureaucracy's facility for stifling generosity must have shown because Moser said, "I'm not one of the bad guys, Mr Samson."

"I worked that out before," I said.

"It's just the way things are."

15

I didn't return to the hospital until the morning. The heavy rain had stopped at last. Impenetrably gray skies were dropping no more than a drizzle.

Sam met me there, curious to see the guy who was at the center of the action. And I was pleased to see that Nurse Matty was on duty again. Or was it still? "Don't you ever get time off?" I asked her.

"I volunteered for a double," she said, "which tells you something about my private life."

"It tells me you're a wonderful, caring person who's probably stockpiling her money in order to open a charitable foundation."

"Me and Bill Gates." She eyed Sam up. "So, who's your friend? Or is this a non-friend too?"

"She is, indeed, a friend. As well as being my daughter."

"The cop?"

"Yes."

"And she's *your* daughter?" Matty tilted her head. "Her mother must be very very beautiful."

I declined to respond. "How's the patient?" I asked.

"He's making me a little uncomfortable, to tell the truth."

"Because of his endless demands for attention and enhanced comforts?"

"Cut up like he is, he should be restless and trying to get more pain relief out of us. But instead he just lies there."

"And that's a problem for you?"

"He watches everyone come and go, and then he smiles a little smile whenever someone takes his blood pressure or fluffs up his pillows."

"And says thank you, I bet."

"Every time. It's creeping me out. I'll be glad when we get a normal patient back in that bed."

"Matty, have you had a personal chat with him?"

"*Personal?* Is that man code for something I don't understand?"

"Asked him about himself, his family?"

"No." She peered at me. "Why?"

"Well, don't, if what you like is normal."

"OK, now you're creeping me out too." She shook her head. "You know where he is."

"Yeah."

"Nice to meet you," she said to Sam and went about her business.

I led Sam to my non-friend.

Wolfgang was not asleep. He gave us a little smile when we came in. "Albert," he said. "And a stranger." He peered at Sam. "Are you two related? Daughter?"

"Thanks for acknowledging my genes," I said. "This is Sam."

"How do you do, Sam."

"Nice to meet you, Mr… Mozart?"

"Just call me Wolfgang." He turned to me. "I thought you told me your daughter is a police officer."

"She is."

He stared at her. "OK, I can see it now. But there's something… more. You're an unusual person, Ms Samson."

"Is that unusual-good or just unusual-different?" Sam asked.

"Good. Definitely good. You will do things in your life."

"No need to butter her up. She's not here to arrest you," I said.

"We'll see how it goes," Sam said. "No promises."

I said, "They're complaining about you out there. They say you should be trying to get more morphine out of them."

"It's only pain," Wolfgang said.

"There have been developments since I was here yesterday."

"Do I want to know?"

"Probably not, but there will be consequences for you." I sat beside Sam to tell the story of the previous evening. As it went on, Wolfgang looked increasingly weary. Weary and unbelieving.

"*Elaine* is responsible for what happened?"

"I don't know how the law will interpret it, but hers was the big bang from which the rest of yesterday's universe followed."

"But *why*? I took her in. I fed her. Her and her child."

"It was about her, Wolfgang, not you."

He absorbed this. "OK. I can see that. I'm thinking narrowly."

"She was desperate to get rid of her boyfriend. She never intended for anyone to get hurt. And, like yourself, she hasn't had a good experience with the police."

He glanced at Sam, who said, "So she went to her best friend. She got the friend to ask Harvey, the boyfriend, what it would take to get him to leave Elaine alone once and for all. Harvey said money."

Wolfgang shook his head slowly, sad about the way human nature plays out. Maybe he was wishing his dad had taken him along to Planet Other.

"So Elaine and the friend hatched up a plan," I said. "The friend told Harvey that you keep a lot of money around the house. Elaine *thought* he'd go to your place alone and that between you and the women there you'd subdue him and he'd be arrested."

I paused while Wolfgang revisited what had happened in his house the previous day. "When I saw the four masked men," he said, "I shouted for all the women to get out. Everyone ran out the back door."

Except for Nicole. I said, "Maybe Harvey smelled some kind of rat when Elaine's friend became cooperative. But for whatever reason he recruited some friends of his own for the visit to your house. Friends willing to rough you up for some easy money."

"All wearing those terrorists' masks." Wolfgang shook his head, looking wearier and wearier.

Sam said, "We have Harvey in custody, Mr Mozart. I hear that he gave up the rest of the 'terrorists' in about five seconds."

"They're sad, silly men," Wolfgang said. "I've been thinking about how they acted when they had me in their car. They were childish and squabbly. And if they needed money so badly, they should just have asked. I'd have given them some."

"That's not how things are expected to work on Planet Earth," I said. "And chances are it was greed rather than need anyway. For which they'll all go down, for assault with deadly weapons."

"I won't press charges."

"What?"

"I won't testify against them. I should have talked more with Elaine. I should have learned more about *her* problems. I should have worked out some way to help her. I could have talked with this Harvey."

"Had him hold your stone and let it make him see the light?"

"You think I'm crazy, don't you?"

"I'd say you are other-worldly, but you'd just agree with me," I said.

Sam said, "Your refusal to testify won't keep them from being charged, Mr Mozart. They'll testify against each other. The medical records here will establish the injuries. They'll plead out.

And they will go to jail. They're dangerous and they need to be prevented from hurting more innocent people."

I said, "Why wouldn't you help punish idiots who are willing to stab people to get a few bucks?"

"Because jail is not an answer. We have a higher percentage of our population in jail than any other country in the world and things like this *still* happen."

"You could ask the judge to give them twenty-five years of community service."

Wolfgang sat up in his bed. "I want to talk to them." He looked at me but then settled on Sam. "Can you make that happen, Officer Samson? I *need* to talk to them. All of them."

16

Sam and I stood in the parking lot before we went our separate ways. "Weird guy, your friend, Wolfgang," she said.

"He's not my friend."

"Why does he want to talk to Harvey and the other idiots?"

"I think he believes he can spread peace on earth, one peace at a time."

"Is he a megalomaniac?"

"He's got this piece of limestone that he thinks has his extra-terrestrial father's handprint on it. Wolfgang believes that people who touch the stone feel better. Maybe even become better people."

"If they do let him talk to Harvey," Sam said, "they won't let him take a lump of stone into the interview room. They'd be afraid your Wolfgang would just whack him on the head with it."

"That'd make *us* feel better, in his place," I said. "But then again you and I are not extra-terrestrials."

"I suppose I should be thankful that you're human, no matter what Mom says."

"She was never *that* beautiful," I said. "It was her brains I went for. But then they ran out."

"Why didn't you tell Wolfgang that he can't run his house as a refuge anymore?"

"Maybe he'll pass his handprint around Children's Services and they'll sign him up and everyone will live happily ever after."

"You think?"

"With him I don't know what to think," I said. "Will Elaine face charges?"

"She and Laurie didn't tell Harvey 'Go stab,' but they provided information knowing it was likely to result in a felony crime. Most judges won't like that much, especially in an election year."

"Maybe Wolfgang will want to fund a high-priced lawyer for her."

"Has he got a lot of money?"

"I have no idea."

"Will you go back in there now and tell him that Elaine might be in trouble?"

"Do you think I should?" I said.

"Maybe for Nicole," Sam said.

"Yeah, all right. Good kid, isn't she?"

"Yeah."

"Like you," I said. And she didn't even smack me for calling her a kid.

EXTRA FRIES

Snow is nice for the first day or two. And for the first inch or two. But for a week and with accumulations in feet? That's just silly. This is Indianapolis, not Vladivostok.

Not that I was suffering. I keep a full fridge. And I live above my mother's luncheonette—*lots* of lovely food there.

My mother was content to stay in. Old by the calendar perhaps, but she doesn't take blizzards as a cue for crochet work. She's got a gym in the basement and during the "weather" she worked out every day. "Best vacation in years," she said to me.

She liked the break but I'm a private investigator. I need people to work things out for. That's what fills my fridge. So when my doorbell rang I was thrilled. I'd swept snow off the stairs to my office every day but hadn't allowed myself to hope. Facts are my business. Hopes don't cut it.

At the door I discovered two men. "Gentlemen, come in. Get warm." I almost pulled on their sleeves.

"Thank you, Albert," said the one I knew.

"Yeah, thanks," the other one said. They both stomped their galoshes on my welcome mat.

"Sorry not to make an appointment," the man I knew said, "but Lenny has an urgent problem."

Lenny was short and quite plump, maybe in his forties. His bright red cheeks made me wonder if he was one of the jolly fat men we hear about.

"Sit." I waved to my Clients' Chair and another nearby.

The man I knew was born Curtis Nelson but he habitually borrowed the names of child prodigies. "Shirley," he said, guessing the question in my mind.

I worked it out about the same time he added, "Temple." A special Oscar when you're seven must qualify you as a prodigy.

"Shirl's parents *sure* had a weird sense of humor," Lenny said.

Which suggested that Shirley hadn't yet "explained" that his father was an alien—the outer space kind. That's what made him feel a kinship with other special people. I'd previously known Shirley as "LeBron" and then "Wolfgang." Whatever.

I said, "Can I get you guys coffee?"

Lenny cleared his throat. "Milk and three sugars."

"Do you have any herbal teas?" Shirley asked.

I left my visitors and headed downstairs to the luncheonette in search of herbals. I wasn't expecting to find Mom but I'd thought Norman, her manager, would be there and maybe a hardy customer or two. However there was just Katerina, a waitress. Tall, dark, handsome, Ukranian, and a stranger to the concept of "smile," she was playing solitaire.

She started to rise but when she saw it was me she sat down again.

"Hiya," I said.

"You want food, I call Norman to cook for you."

"I'll manage."

"You are not your mother. You should not cook. No insurance." She glared like a Rottweiler guarding the griddle.

I ignored her and looked for teas. I found peppermint, took one teabag and held it up so Katerina could see. Then I showed her a quarter, put it on the counter, and headed for my stairs.

She said, "Tea is one dollar."

I said nothing.

"What about tip?" she called as I passed through the curtains.

I gave Lenny his sweet coffee. Handing Shirley his tea I asked, "Who's my prospective client here?"

"I'm just the facilitator," Shirley said. "Lenny came to my refuge."

"Refuge?"

"I have a basement downtown now. I help people to help themselves. That's why I bought Lenny here."

How my helping Lenny amounted to Lenny helping himself wasn't immediately obvious but I turned to him. "What's your problem?"

"Where should I start?"

"At the beginning?"

He cleared his throat. "Well, my wife quit smoking a few years ago."

Was it going to be an autobiography? Well, it was snowing and these were my first visitors for ages. "Uh huh."

"Before that we'd been talking about maybe moving somewhere, which I really wanted to do. But she then got broody and decided she wouldn't move unless it was closer to her mom."

These details seemed important to him. I drank some coffee.

"We've already got the one kid and Emma's thirty-nine. Well, she was thirty-six then, which might've meant something historically. But that is too young to be desperate these days. I really like history. I like to give things a historical perspective."

He stopped. I thought he'd sample his own coffee but all he did was warm his hands on it. I tried to prime the pump. "Yes?"

"But Em decided if she was going to have another kid, then this time she'd do it right. So she gave up the smoking."

"Did something go wrong with her first pregnancy?"

"No. Well, who knows? Nowadays Cory dresses in black like one of those Goth kids and only listens to depressing music. Em smoked and drank when she was pregnant with him. And Cory's never been big, which could just be my genes, but all the rules for pregnancy are so different now."

"And?"

"She never got pregnant again. All she got was fat."

"Which can happen when you quit smoking. Along with being irritable."

"Irritable? Who can tell with her? Em *always* knows what she wants and pity whoever gets in the way."

"But she put on weight?"

"And she couldn't let *that* go on. So a couple of months ago she put us on a diet."

"Us?"

"Her and me. Don't know if you noticed, I carry some weight myself. Not from smoking, but because I screwed up my knee." He patted his right knee. "I used to be a jock and…"

"You gained weight, which can happen with a knee. So you went on a diet with her."

"She *put* us on a diet. I never wanted to. I like my meat and potatoes."

"So you *didn't* go on the diet."

"I didn't want to, but I did. It's more than your life is worth to say no to Em."

"Lenny, I'm not seeing how your story leads you to me."

"Oh, you were Shirley's suggestion."

"I'll thank him later but please get to the point."

"Cause you're a busy guy. I get it. So the point is that Em doesn't do things by halves. She decided to lose weight, and she *was* getting a little porky. But she decided, and she put me on the diet with her. Me, I'd rather just buy bigger clothes." He paused and I waited.

He said, "This diet—it's killing me."

Kill is not a word I use lightly though many people do. I glanced at Shirley. He lifted a finger to tell me to stick with it.

"This diet, I'm telling you. It's killing me," Lenny said. "OK, here's the thing. Five weeks ago Em caught me cheating."

"Cheating?"

"On the diet. I wasn't losing weight, see. I was eating all this stuff—salad and skinless chicken and broccoli. And *she* was losing weight fast—still is, three, four pounds a week—but I wasn't losing any."

"And…?"

"First she upped the stakes. She picked everything that went into my lunch box and weighed me twice a day instead of once. But I still didn't lose anything. So one day she followed me. Can you believe that? Her own husband for sixteen years and she *follows* me."

"Where did you lead?"

"Peppy's."

Peppy Grill is a few blocks from Mom's place, the last diner in Indianapolis that's open 24/7. "Your wife caught you coming out of Peppy with ketchup on your face, or what?"

"She caught me tucking into a cheeseburger deluxe with double fries and onion rings."

"And?"

"She exploded. It was 'How could you do this to me?' and 'A fat man like you is repulsive' and 'After all the work I put in on the diet for you.'"

"In front of everybody?"

"Peppy's was packed." Lenny's plump cheeks seemed to collapse at the memory. "I'd never seen Em like that before. It *really* scared me. Even at home I couldn't shut her up. It was the worst betrayal in the world. If would have been better if I'd killed JFK."

"Did you kill JFK?" I asked.

"What? Oh. I've never been to Texas."

"But eventually Emma did stop?"

"Because of Cory. She was still at it when he came in from school. He started to cry and that's what finally did it."

"Cory's close to his mother?"

"Not since he became a Goth. Usually he'd rather die than show his feelings. It shocked her. That he cared enough to cry."

I leaned back. "Lenny, so far we have you on a diet you didn't want to be on, and we have you getting caught with a cheeseburger, and we have you getting shouted at and making your kid cry."

"There's more," Shirley said.

Lenny nodded. "So I swore up and down that I would stay on the diet. And I've been losing weight."

"Congratulations."

"But I shouldn't be."

"It's science, Lenny," I said. "It's like Mr Micawber. Nineteen hundred calories in, two thousand out, a happy man."

"Because I'm still cheating."

"What?"

"On the diet. I go to Peppy's for lunch every weekday. That's more often than I did before. I have the Deluxe Platter."

"But your wife makes you lunch."

"When she calls at lunchtime I say I'm eating what she packed. Sometimes she puts some little surprise, like a flower, in the box so I look, to confirm I found it."

"But you don't eat the lunch?"

"Maybe the apple. I'm getting to like apples."

"And instead you eat at Peppy."

"Yeah. I don't have much time, but Rhonda knows what I want when I walk in the door."

"Rhonda?"

"The afternoon waitress. I always have the Deluxe Platter with double fries. It was maybe three times a week when I wasn't losing weight but now it's five times and I *am* losing weight. Three or four pounds each of the last four weeks."

"And you're complaining?"

"Because my wife is poisoning me, Mr Samson. I'm sure of it."

2

Intentional poisoning is rare these days, even by wives. I said, "Lots of things can cause weight-loss, Lenny."

"I know. And I went to my doctor for a full diagnostic. I work for an HMO and I get a really good health plan."

"And?"

"She couldn't find anything wrong. She said to check my lifestyle and look for environmental factors."

"What exercise do you get?"

"I sit all day. And it's *really* boring, but when you've majored in French history you take whatever you can get, you know? But it puts food on the table. Only it used to be *real* food."

"No sports?"

"Sometimes I have to walk a block after I drive to work. Honestly, Mr Samson, there's no legitimate reason for what's happening. I'm really scared."

"What's your wife's attitude now?"

"She weighs me. I'm losing weight. That's all she cares about. Nothing else, not my happiness, not nothing. If she wanted a baby now she'd go to an adoption agency." He shook his head sadly.

"You only cheat on weekdays?"

"I only get away from her to go to work or when she works. If I visit my parents she comes too even though she hates them. And we never stay for meals anymore. Mom slips me some chocolate but I get scared Em will smell it on my breath."

"So your only freedom is lunchtime at Peppy."

"Yes."

"With Rhonda."

"Rhonda was there when Emma threw her fit and she sympathizes. I sit down, I get a big smile, and a few minutes later the food comes. I don't have to say a word and she doesn't have to say it back."

"How would you describe your relationship with Rhonda, Lenny?"

"I've never once seen her outside of Peppy. I'm not sure she knows my name. But when I see her it does make me happy, I have to say that."

"Lenny, if you're so unhappy with Emma, why don't you move out or get a divorce?"

"I'd lose my son. I talked to a lawyer. The mother's rights are really powerful, especially if I wanted us to move to my parents' house." Lenny leaned back for a moment. "The thing is, I hate my job and my parents are doing really well. They say I should come work for them."

"What do they do?"

"Nowadays they grow ingredients for aromatherapy treatments. Wholesale supply. They've got this farm up near Camden. But Em says that she'd rather die than live out in the country like that."

"Bit extreme," I said.

"Em doesn't do compromise. At first I thought it was because her family was military but she's worse than any of them. Things are her way or they're the wrong way. Plus, she and her folks never liked that my parents both did time in prison."

I raised my eyebrows.

"Just for growing and selling a little pot. Dad did four years but Mom did six."

"She was the ringleader?"

"Mom doesn't do good behavior."

I noted the use of the present tense. And the secret chocolate.

He said, "I'm their only child and Cory's their only grandchild. They want me to be closer and I'd love that. But Em won't hear of it."

"OK, you're not going to leave her, which was the original question. Here's another. What, exactly, do you want *me* to do?"

"If I bring you samples of what she feeds me, you could get a lab to see what poison she's using."

"You could find a lab for yourself."

Lenny shook his head. "I couldn't do it at work without someone asking why. And if I did it from home Em would find out for sure."

"OK," I said, "suppose I find out that Emma *is* poisoning you. What would you do? Sic the cops on her?"

"I… I don't really know yet."

This bit of indecision made me wonder if he'd thought his story through. Or even believed it. But if he wanted to pay me for nothing much why should I complain? I took five hundred dollars as a retainer. He didn't blink.

"What I want," Lenny said, "is for her to let me be whatever *I* want to be. I *hate* the damn salads."

"The Egyptians thought lettuce was an aphrodisiac," I said.

"I don't," he said.

3

Lenny would bring the food samples to me. Once I had results from a lab I would report to him on his cell phone.

As he prepared to leave I asked Shirley to stay behind.

"Is that all right, Lenny?" Shirley asked. "Are you going home now?"

"Em's at work. I'm going to Peppy for a snack."

I said, "The luncheonette downstairs is open. Avoid the snow?"

"I'd rather go to Peppy."

Shirley and I watched him wrap up and head out.

When he'd gone I said, "Does Lenny have some other agenda? If all he wants is lab tests on his food, you could have found him a lab with a couple of phonecalls. And why is he insisting it's poison anyway? Why not a laxative?"

"Don't you *want* a paying client?" Shirley asked.

"If he *is* being poisoned he should go to the cops," I said. "If he isn't he should go to a shrink."

"Psychiatrists don't know squat," Shirley said with feeling.

I guess he knew.

Then he asked, "Is the luncheonette downstairs really open?"

Katerina was no longer playing cards. She was refilling ketchup bottles.

"Paying customers," I said.

"Take seat. I bring menu."

"I know the menu and I'll share my knowledge. Meanwhile we want a peppermint tea and a black coffee."

She faced us and glared. "Take seat. I bring menu."

Shirley said, "Let's take a seat."

I followed him to a window table. We had a good view of the piles left by the snowplows.

Moments later Katerina slapped down two menus. "If you want cooked, I must call Norman. So, what you want?"

"Time to consider our options," I said. The only way to deal with bullies is to stand up to them.

"Even though you know menu?" She scowled. "I wait."

"Where are you from?" Shirley asked.

"Where there are not so much stupid people."

"Is there a pie you'd recommend?"

"All pie is two days old but chocolate cake Norman makes this morning. Very good, I think."

"Then chocolate cake for me," Shirley said, "and a peppermint tea."

Katerina gave a sharp nod. She turned her glare on me.

"A black coffee, please, Katerina."

She pivoted and left.

Shirley watched her. "She has a nice voice."

"Pity about what she uses it to say."

He continued to watch her.

"Shirley…? Are you interested?"

"Maybe."

"What about when you tell her your name is Shirley Temple?"

"I have this feeling that she'll understand."

4

I wanted to get more information about Lenny but Shirley's mind was elsewhere. "Albert, do you know if Katerina is single?"

"Why don't you give me five hundred bucks to find out?"

"What? Oh."

I gave up and left him to it.

Back upstairs I settled to earning Lenny's retainer. A search showed plenty of commercial labs available in Indy. Great if you want to test for asbestos, mold, lead, radon, pesticides, bacteria, air, or fungus. But no ad offered to test for poisoned pasta. So I hit the phone.

The first guy I explained what I wanted to said, "Is this a joke?"

But at the second lab a woman answered and she found the situation entirely plausible. "Making her husband just fade away... Acting out the dream? I'm only joking. Hehe."

She was Luci with an "i". Various possibilities occurred to her after I explained what I knew. "It needn't be a poison, but stimulants would suppress the appetite altogether, so they're out. And weight-loss drugs have side effects that your client would have noticed."

"I wondered about laxatives."

"How frequently is he doing a number two?"

"I have no idea."

"A poison could irritate the gastrointestinal tract, cause weight-loss, and do it by moving food through quickly—the same as laxatives or the weight-loss drugs."

"OK..."

"But if it were me..." She paused.

"Luci?"

"Sorry, just daydreaming. Right, if it were me, I'd probably use a common poison rather than a drug. You can get drugs without a prescription but there are still receipts and packaging to give the game away and make a suspicious husband do something like hire a private detective. Hehe."

"You're more inclined to be a poison lady than a drug lady?"

"Definitely."

"What 'common' poisons are we talking about?"

"Strychnine, say, or arsenic or antimony. Any of them could have the effect. The right dose to achieve weight-loss but not death might take some experimentation though. Has the wife in question lost any previous husbands to malnutrition?"

"Not that I know about."

"Or does she have some kind of medical or scientific background?"

"Dunno."

We could have talked cheerfully for long time but Luci got called away.

There was nothing more I could do on Lenny's case in the office so I decided to go downstairs and claim my coffee refill. I never expected to find Shirley still there. He was standing close behind Katerina as she played the pinball machine.

Not my business. If he *was* the son of an alien father he was as likely to find love with alien Katerina as with anyone. I went back upstairs, dressed to go outside, and headed for Peppy Grill.

5

What should have been a five minute walk took me half an hour. There are people in the world who *love* the snow. I'm not one of them.

By the time I clambered up the steps to Peppy, Lenny had gone. I saw only two people. One was a heavyset guy in a booth. The other was a woman behind the counter.

She was mid-thirties, tall and very slim. Her dark hair was gathered under a net. She greeted me with a smile that made me feel like family. "Welcome, stranger. Come in from the cold." It was a simple message in the context but it was delivered with conviction.

I took a stool at the counter.

"Have you come far?" she asked.

"It felt like it."

"Well, don't forget, in the cold you need extra calories."

"Or I can eat what I usually do and lose weight."

"You don't need to lose weight."

"Yes I do."

"Not *need.* You should never lose weight unless *you* want to. Don't let anybody force it on you."

Less than two minutes and we were at the heart of Lenny's problem. What an efficient investigator I am... "Sounds like you're speaking from experience."

"My ex-husband couldn't *bear* it when I got fat."

"The last thing you are is fat."

"I was. Well, plump."

"Do you regret losing the weight?"

"I regret losing it because *he* wanted me to."

"That doesn't sound like a nice story."

She sighed. "My ex gave me this stuff. But even after I got down to what the charts say is 'normal' he kept criticizing me and giving me more."

"What did he give you?"

"Some experimental drug. He works at Loftus and *said* he pulled strings to get me on a trial." Loftus is an international pharmaceuticals company based in Indy.

"Oh."

"I didn't *want* to take some untested chemical but he swore it was safe. Then I had to keep taking the pills because I could never lose enough weight to suit him."

"Isn't that abuse?"

"Eventually I figured that out for myself." She shook her head with what I took to be self-disgust. "The tragedy is that I let him do it to me for so long. Even now I can hardly bring myself to eat."

"What's this drug called?"

"He said they call it AR 52."

"Could not wanting to eat now be a side-effect?"

"How do I know?" She rubbed her forehead and looked distressed. "I don't want to talk about that anymore. It gives me shivers even now."

"And the last thing anyone needs in this weather is extra shivers. Well, I'll have coffee and some calories, please."

"What kind of calories would you like?"

"Surprise me."

So she surprised me by taking on the challenge. She cut a slice of cherry pie and paused, examining my expression. Then she put the pie in a microwave. While it was being nuked she scooped some ice cream.

When the dish was in front of me, she asked, "How'd I do?"

"What's the ice cream?"

"Butter pecan."

"My mother's favorite."

She nodded, looking sage.

"Just what I would have asked for." Or close enough. "Are you a witch, Rhonda?"

She froze. "How do you know my name? Did Brad send you?"

"Who's Brad? The ex?"

"Not your business," she said. "Who're *you?*"

"Albert." I smiled and tried to look unthreatening. "A guy I'm doing some work for comes in here and he told me about you. Nothing creepy or sinister. He just likes you."

"I know this guy?"

"I don't know if you know his name."

"Try me."

"I can't do that without his permission."

"What does he eat?"

Would it be a breach of client confidentiality to call him Mr Deluxe Platter with double fries? Probably. "I'll ask next time I see him. But he knows your name and said very nice things about you. I even wondered if he was going to leave his wife for you."

"I do not socialize with men who have wives, Albert," she said coldly. "What kind of work is it that you do?"

"I'm a detective."

"Brad *did* send you." She shivered.

"No. I swear it's not Brad. Look, I'm just a local guy—my mom owns Bud's Dugout." The luncheonette was named after my late father. "I work out of an office above it."

"And what kind of detecting are you doing for this customer of mine?"

"I can't tell you that either."

"So I talk to you but you don't talk to me?"

"Sorry. It's the rules. So I'm going to eat now before the warm pie melts all the ice cream and spoils this wonderful combination."

Rhonda was never likely to provide information that was relevant to Lenny's case but I did wonder if Lenny might be smitten with her like Shirley was with Katerina. Falling for a woman who brings the food you like is an understandable phenomenon.

But all I could do now for my client was wait for him to bring *me* food. However on my way home I went through the luncheonette. Katerina was alone. Playing solitaire.

I didn't *intend* to say anything. But she said, "I see how you look."

"Snowy?"

"Dishes are washed. Griddle is scraped. Mustard is full. I can't help no customers."

"Did I complain?"

"Your face says, 'She is playing cards again and for this she is being paid.'"

"That's not my business, Katerina."

"Doggone tootin'."

But I went over. "How long did Shirley stay?"

"He stays long enough to be late for somewhere else. Not long enough to find nerve to ask me for date. But he tells there is a diet client for you. Your mother will be happy you have work. Or does fat Lenny not pay?"

"He pays."

"And you will take much time to solve his fat so you take much of his money?"

"I will solve his fat as quickly as I can."

"Good honor, but bad business."

"That's me in a nutshell," I said. "That's—"

"I know what is a nutshell. I think only that it contains one nut inside."

I turned to head for my stairs.

She said, "Do you not think this fat Lenny makes secret exercise so he can see his burger love woman who is on the side like extra fries?"

I wished I'd asked Rhonda how she'd feel about being someone's burger love woman. "He says he isn't doing that."

"If he hires, you always trust?"

The truth is that clients often lie, but I opted to stay silent.

"I think this fat Lenny must do secrets he doesn't tell you. How else does he get thin? You must make more questions for fat Lenny. Because to lose weight with double fries is not biological."

"You are so young, Katerina, and yet so wise."

"It is gift and also curse."

She put a red ten on a black jack. I headed to my office.

I thought about calling Lenny. But he was due to come to me once he had collected his food samples and any more questions could wait till then.

If I really wanted to crack the case I should talk with Emma. I went as far as looking up their landline number. But I couldn't think of what to say even if she answered.

So instead I fell asleep.

I dreamt I was walking barefoot. My feet got cold and sank into a snowy hole. I feared there were malevolent icy creatures at the bottom of the hole.

6

Lenny knocked on my door at about eight, face red from the cold. After he banged snow off his boots he pulled five plastic bags from an inside pocket. "The green one is a salad. Grilled turkey breast with mushrooms and onions is in number two. Three is cauliflower. Four is fruit salad. Five is the diet lemonade that's all I'm allowed to drink at home except water."

"Grilled turkey? Cauliflower?"

He shuddered. "You know the best meat I ever had? Meat I shot myself." He looked me in the eye.

"Is Emma in danger from you, Lenny?"

"Of course not."

"Do you keep guns in the house?"

"I used to but I moved them up to my folks when Cory painted his bedroom black."

"You think Cory is dangerous?"

Something soft passed through Lenny's expression as he thought of his son. "No, not for a single minute. But Em and I talked about it. And she wanted the guns gone."

"Because of the black?"

"He doesn't bring friends to the house. He's on the computer all the time. Em says the parents are the last to know. So I moved the guns. A rifle I had from when I was a kid myself, and a bedside .22." Lenny shook his head again, this time slowly and sadly. "Emma can be such a hardass."

I piled the sample-bags together, ready to store in my fridge. "I'll get these to the lab tomorrow." I didn't intend to dig my car out from what the snowplows had piled on it, but I did have a telephone. There was bound to be a frost-proof courier who'd do the job.

"Great."

"A few more questions, OK?"

"What?"

"You met Emma at work but what did she do before that? Does she have any scientific background."

"She majored in biology. Why?"

"The technician at the lab asked. Calculating poison doses can be tricky."

"Oh." His face registered shock. "That makes it so *real*."

"Lenny, if you didn't think it was real, why the hell did you come to me?"

"I know." He closed his eyes for a moment.

"There are poisons that can cause weight-loss, but avoiding life-loss at the same time isn't easy."

"Em's real organized."

I moved on. "I was in Peppy Grill today."

"Yeah?"

"I'd like to go back and talk more with Rhonda. Maybe about when Emma caught you there. Is that OK?"

"I guess."

"OK, something else. Since you started losing weight have you noticed any body changes related to your digestion? Stomach aches. Abdominal pain. Bowel movements. Acid reflux."

"I… It's embarrassing."

"And you're blushing. But I need to know."

He took a breath. "I get pains in my gut but I always do when she shouts at me."

"She's shouted at you a lot over the years?"

"Em… She's emphatic."

"Anything else?"

"Well, I do more number twos than I used to."

I nodded.

He sat, waiting.

His passivity was beginning to annoy me. "You raised the subject of poison here, and presumably you hired me to reduce the chance of your dying. Tell me about any and all changes that you're aware off."

"Not digestive. Headaches. I get headaches." He touched himself above the right eye.

"Sharp? Dull? Constant? Intermittent?"

"About ten minutes after I wake up it starts. Then it's there most of the time."

"Anything else?"

"No."

"OK. Something different. Why did you go to Shirley's refuge?"

"For help. I was worried."

"Not to your doctor? Or a friend? Or your boss?"

"I was walking around. I saw a poster. It seemed like a good idea."

"Walking around? I thought you didn't get any exercise."

"That's not enough to count. And I get out of the house whenever I can. Honestly, Mr Samson, I'm *really* scared."

7

The evening forecasters suggested the snow might ease off by the morning.

It didn't.

However it takes more than a blizzard to stop commercial activity in a capitalist hotspot like Indianapolis, Indiana. I found a courier willing to pick up Lenny's plastic bags and transport them to the lab's northwest address, for only triple the usual rate. But first I confirmed that Luci with an i was at work.

"Where else would I be?" she asked as if she lived on the premises.

"Sorry to doubt your commitment," I said. "The samples should be with you by eleven. When can you start on them?"

"As soon as they get here, because I multi-task. That's something women do that maybe you haven't heard of. But report back? Depends what I find and how many tests it takes to find it."

Speaking of what she *might* find, I mentioned the experimental drug that Brad had pushed on Rhonda. Emma met Lenny at work, an HMO. So she might have connections at Loftus. Not likely but I didn't want Luci to miss anything for want of looking.

"What chemical family is this AR 52 in?" she asked.

I laughed.

She laughed.

We hung up.

After the courier left I decided to take a break. But before I even got up from my desk the phone rang.

"Hello?" I said, thinking of day-old chocolate cake.

"Who is this?" a woman asked.

I didn't recognize the voice. "If you're selling something, move down your list."

"I'm not selling anything."

"Good, because I'm not buying."

I was about to hang up when she said, "Are you married?"

"*What*?"

"Or with a girl-friend? It's just I was expecting a woman to answer the phone."

"Any particular reason?"

"Because I found this number in my husband's pants pocket. So who *are* you?"

"I'll tell you if you tell me first."

She thought about that for a moment. Then she hung up.

I checked, but she'd withheld her number.

So I thought about it for a moment. Husbands who might have written down my phone number recently made a very short list. I deduced that I'd just been talking with Emma.

Katerina had three customers in the luncheonette—an elderly couple who held hands and a small guy in many layers of clothing who had a knapsack with a sleeping bag attached. He was either an Xtreme camper or he was homeless. I wondered if he knew about Shirley's refuge.

With customers in, Norman was at his station, griddling. I don't get on with Norman. I wanted good thinking time rather than bad badinage. So I turned around, got my coat and headed to Peppy.

While I walked I mulled over Emma's call. Pity I hadn't been quick enough to ask, "Are you poisoning this husband of yours, yes or no?"

But she'd expected a woman to answer. Did she fear Lenny's cheating might go beyond food?

The only woman I knew of in Lenny's life was Rhonda. She'd dismissed ever having a relationship with a married man, but that mightn't keep Lenny from trying.

Rhonda remembered me. "Back again," she said, not exactly radiating warmth.

I made my way to the stool I'd used before, the only customer in the place.

"I was thinking about you," she said as she came over. "If you're in here, you're detecting, not eating, right?"

"Can't a guy do both?"

"The eating I can promise to help you with."

"Coffee and some chocolate cake?"

She nodded and put both in front of me. "And for the detecting?"

"The guy I'm working for doesn't mind my telling you that he's Mr Deluxe Platter. Comes in here weekday afternoons?"

"Lenny?"

Who *said* he wasn't sure she knew his name… "His wife came in here once."

"And shouted the place down because he was supposed to be on a diet." She shivered. "I felt awful for him."

I believed her sincerity and sympathy. "And you'd been through bad diet times yourself."

"But never in public. And this woman, she went on and on and on."

I took a bite of the cake and sipped from my coffee.

"Cake OK?"

"Better than OK." Better than Norman's. I was pleased in a small-minded way. "With your experience of being bullied about dieting, you must've really felt sorry for Lenny."

"Even now I give him extra fries. It's his own damn business what he eats. No one has the right to shame him for it."

"I was thinking about Brad and the AR 52."

"Yeah?"

"You like Lenny, don't you?"

"Sure."

"Well, he's worried, because he's losing a lot of weight even though he's eating here every weekday. So I was thinking, wondering if maybe you were giving him a helping hand."

Rhonda's eyes narrowed as she got my point. "You think I'd put some leftover AR 52 into Lenny's food?"

"Maybe, if you liked him. If it helped him keep from being humiliated again. You know the stuff works."

"Drug a customer's food? You think I'd give him extra fries and then doctor them? Why? Because I love him? Or because I'm a sicko like Brad?"

"Maybe because you sympathize with his situation?"

"Is that what *he* thinks?"

"No."

She studied me. "You know what *I* think?"

"What?"

"That you should get yourself out of here before I start banging plates on your head."

I looked into her eyes.

I left.

8

I believed Rhonda, so my bright idea was dim. And worse than having been wrong, I'd insulted her, a genuinely nice woman. Not my best morning's work.

But no alternative idea occurred to me as I walked back to Bud's. Except that I still wanted cake and coffee. A bite and a sip weren't enough.

Inside the only customer was the homeless guy. I took a seat by the window.

Katerina came over and took my order without a scowl or a growl. Was she softening? Could she guess I was feeling guilty about another waitress? Either way I was encouraged to ask, "Yesterday, did Shirley give you the address of his refuge?"

"You think I am needing refuge?" Waitresses can be *so* touchy…

"I think maybe the homeless guy over there could use it."

She turned to look. "He is a homeless?"

I nodded.

She went to the counter, picked up a card, and offered it to the homeless guy after refilling his coffee. They talked, but the card didn't change hands.

When she brought my food I said, "He didn't want refuge?"

"He not find his spectacles so I read it to him. But you know what I think?"

"What?"

"I think he is a homeless who cannot read. Through two nets he slips in your home of the brave."

"Maybe Shirley *can* help him."

"Have you found the secret exercise of this Fat Lenny?"

"He still says he doesn't exercise."

"And you believe?"

"I believe."

"Perhaps you hire detective to follow and find out for sure. With his money, of course."

I was about to laugh but she'd already left. I watched as she put a piece of cherry pie on a plate and took it to the homeless guy. He accepted it with obvious pleasure. One less net that he was slipping through today. Katerina came back to me.

I said, "Well done."

"Otherwise we throw away. It is nothing off my nose." Then, "Is he also rich, this Fat Lenny?"

"I don't know."

She frowned. It was clearly essential information that I'd failed to gather.

"He has a job, enough cash to hire me, and his parents run a successful business."

"Check who is inheritance," she said with a firm nod.

Luci called just before one-thirty. She began by saying the word, "Arsenic."

It seemed incredible for the 21st Century.

"I'm running a lot of tests," Luci said, "but one of the first results was positive for arsenic. On the turkey—not in the other samples."

"Wow."

"It's a good poison choice. If it were me I might use the same."

"Why?" Was this *really* a 21st Century conversation?

"The beauty of arsenic is that it never breaks down. So if your poisoner—the wife, right?—if she had some in the garage it would still work perfectly even if it was years old. She wouldn't have to allow for deterioration."

"Why would she have some in the garage?"

"Well, it used to be in rat poisons. And some wood preservatives. Then there's leather tanning and semiconductors. It's cool stuff."

"Cool?"

"But you said the husband's losing weight?"

"For more than a month. Three or four pounds a week."

"I'm surprised, because there wasn't much arsenic in the sample--more like what 'ladies' in the Italian Renaissance took to give themselves pink cheeks. If this was his daily dose, I wouldn't have expected symptoms beyond maybe a red face and a headache. Nothing more serious unless he's tiny. What's his body weight?"

"He isn't tiny—which is why the diet is an issue. Are you sure the arsenic you found couldn't have occurred naturally?"

"Oh, it definitely occurred unnaturally."

"And you're surprised about the weight-loss."

"But people are different. Or maybe the wife went easy on this meal because she gave him too much the day before. If you want a better picture, give me samples from all his meals over a couple of weeks."

"I'll put that to him."

"Or give me some hair. I can work out how much arsenic's already accumulated in his body. Unless your guy is bald."

"He's not bald."

"Well, I'm also happy to testify in court about my findings, but I charge a whole day for that."

Had she gone to the same business school as Katerina?

I told her that I'd consult my client. But first I consulted myself.

The turkey Emma had prepared for Lenny *was* poisoned. And it wasn't accidental. Yet if it was his daily dose, Lenny shouldn't be losing weight. Might Emma be dosing him little but often? Or might she know more than Luci about arsenic as a dietary aid? Maybe she had experience using it on herself? *She'd* lost significant weight since starting the diet.

But if she was feeding *herself* arsenic, why hadn't she given it to Lenny from the beginning?

I had new information, but not new knowledge.

But I needed to report the information to my client, and quickly. And maybe go to the cops?

I called Lenny's cell. "Where are you?"

"It's my lunch hour." Then, "I've only just gotten here."

So, at Peppy. "Look, I have some information from the lab. Shall I come over?"

He hesitated before he said, "Yeah. OK. I guess so."

"Order a coffee for me. And I warn you now, I'll be stealing one of your fries."

It didn't occur to me till I was trudging down Virginia Avenue that maybe eating *any* food prepared for him was not that good an idea.

9

I found Lenny in a booth surrounded by the foods he loved more than his wife's good opinion. There was, indeed, an extra cup of coffee across from him. But no greeting from Rhonda.

Lenny had cut his double cheeseburger into thirds. The third he was working on was loaded with condiments. He looked happy.

"Two fries, no more," he said once he'd swallowed. "And one *small* onion ring."

"Thank you, but it's not professional to take the food out of clients' mouths. Sorry to have joked about serious matters."

He nodded with unconcern. He took two fries for himself, along with an onion ring nobody could have called small. "You have information?"

"You *are* being poisoned."

He stopped mid-mouthful.

"There was arsenic on the turkey you gave me last night."

He swallowed. "Arsenic? Really?"

"The lab technician called a few minutes ago. She isn't finished but she thought I'd want to know now and I thought you'd want to know now."

"I would. I do. *Arsenic*?"

"Not much—not a toxic amount—but it didn't get there accidentally."

"Oh my God," he said.

"However the technician also said she didn't think there was enough arsenic to cause you to lose weight like you have."

He frowned. "What's that mean?"

"If what was on the turkey was your daily dose, you shouldn't suffer more than flushed cheeks and maybe a headache." I looked at his pink cheeks. And he'd told me about headaches before. "What else does Emma cook for you? Bringing more samples for testing would let the technician gauge more accurately how much arsenic you're being fed."

"Keep *eating* food with arsenic on it?"

"Or the technician could analyze some of your hair instead. From hair she can estimate how much you've eaten and how long you've been eating it."

Lenny picked up a fry.

I said, "This is shocking information, I know. What do you want to do from here?"

I waited.

But the next person to speak was Rhonda. "Lenny?" She held a coffeepot. "How are we doing here?"

His torpor vanished. He turned with a big smile and held out his mug. She steadied it with one hand, grazing his fingers, and poured.

When she was gone Lenny returned his gaze to his burger. "I'll call you," he said. "About what I decide to do."

He was telling me to go.

He bit.

I went.

10

Lenny had shown shock when his unlikely suspicion was confirmed but the news certainly hadn't put him off his food.

Maybe he thought best while he was eating—his meals at Peppy *were* important to him. But were his slight contacts with Rhonda's fingers significant? Or was a professionally suspicious guy making a snowdrift out of a few flakes?

My brain felt like a snowflake dome that was being constantly shaken so I couldn't see clearly what was inside.

The first of my late afternoon business calls came at about four-thirty. It was from Lenny. "I've decided to confront Emma tonight. I want you there. Can you come to my house?"

"Me? Why?"

"I want you to tell her that a lab found arsenic on the turkey."

"She wouldn't believe you?"

"I'd prefer you to confirm it. As a neutral voice."

"Well, my car's under a snowdrift but if you don't mind paying for a cab..."

"I'll pay. And I've made an appointment with my lawyer. I'll want you to come to that too. Tomorrow at eleven."

"Your *lawyer?*"

"Emma's feeding me *arsenic*, Mr Samson. That can't go on, whatever the consequences. And you'll need to tell the lawyer what lab you used. It *was* a reputable lab, wasn't it?"

"The internet says so."

"And I want them to test my hair to show how long she's been doing it. Does it take a lot of hair?"

"I'll ask."

"Great. Six-thirty at mine." He hung up.

His *lawyer?* Not the cops?

The second call was from Shirley. "No," I said when he identified himself, "I won't act as go-between for you with Katerina. You'll have be big and bwave and ask her out yourself."

"You think I should?"

"Next question, please."

"Has she said anything about me?"

"Next question, please."

"Lenny just called. He said there was *arsenic* in his food."

If my client was spreading the word, there was no point in my silence. "The lab found it in a turkey sample."

"He told me he's going to confront his wife. He said you're coming. He wants me there too. 'For support.'"

"What support can you give him?"

"Advice? Reassurance?"

"How about a bed at the refuge?"

"That too, I guess."

"But for him or for her?"

A lawyer, a private eye and half an alien. But still no cops.

The third business call came before five. It was from Luci with an i. "I'm glad you called," I said. "Can you email me a formal statement about your test results?"

"I'm just about to do that."

"And my client wants you to test his hair. How much do you need?"

She told me about hair quantities and what the tests would cost. Then she said, "I finished the rest of my tests a little while ago, and there's something you should know. It's in the email but I can summarize while I'm sending it to you."

"I know," I said. "It's called multi-tasking."

I made the fourth business call myself. To Lenny's cell because I wanted to go through Luci's report with him. But his phone was off. I left a message asking him to call me back.

11

Lenny and Emma lived just off Miami in a new downtown development. Miami had been plowed so the cab dropped me outside only a few minutes after six-thirty.

A woman who had to be Emma opened the door. She was a bit above average height, with curly blonde hair, and although she wasn't thin she was hardly fat. She was, however, frowning.

"Another one," she said. "Just who are *you?*"

"Albert Samson. Lenny invited me."

"Well I *suppose* you had better come up and get on with whatever he's up to. But he knows I don't like surprises."

"Does he surprise you often?"

"He knows I don't *like* surprises."

She led me down a hall and into a living room that was sparely, but stylishly, furnished. Shirley sat on a straight wooden chair. He looked uncomfortable. I doubted that was the chair's fault.

Lenny stood next to him, looking even less at ease than his guest.

At the end of the room I caught a glimpse of a dark-haired boy peering out from a doorway. Cory?

Emma faced everyone. "Well, Leonard, here's another cog in whatever crackpot machine you're making. Did you remember to get beer and chips?" Not waiting for an answer she turned to me. "Are you housetrained enough to sit for whatever you do?" She gestured to a couch and another wooden chair.

I expected Lenny to speak. But he was dithering. That irritated me. I stayed where I was. "Now we're here, what's the agenda, Lenny?"

"Agenda?" Emma said with a snort. "Is this a *meeting*? My Leonard couldn't organize a *meeting* in a *meat* factory."

It was time for Lenny to man up and even he knew it. So, pink cheeks blazing, he cleared his throat a couple of times.

"Get on with it," Emma said.

Lenny said, "Em, as everyone here knows, two months ago you put me on a diet."

"These strangers know our business?" Her contemptuous glance took in Shirley and me. "*We* went on a diet. Which Leonard cheated on—until he was caught."

"Em…" Lenny said.

"And don't you make that face at me. They ought to know the *truth* about you."

"I didn't want to diet."

"It was for your own good."

The dam began to break. "And was it for my own good that you started poisoning me?"

Emma was surprised by that. But though she didn't like surprises, she was quick enough to respond. "*Poison* you? With healthy food? It's those greasy cheeseburgers you love so much that were the poison."

"I…" Lenny turned to me. "Mr Samson is a private detective."

"He's *what*?"

"And he arranged for a really reliable lab to test the food you gave me last night."

Emma was startled into a silence.

"Mr Samson? You have a report."

"I do. And I tried to call you about it but you never called me back."

"I… I was busy."

Emma regained her voice. "What kind of 'private detective' could *you* possibly be?"

I don't like bullies. "Sit down," I said sharply, pointing to the couch, "and be quiet."

Bullies only understand one language. She sat. She made a face but she shut up.

I said, "Last night Lenny brought me samples of the food you served him for dinner."

She took a breath but I raised a finger. "This morning I sent those samples to a lab. This afternoon the senior lab technician reported that she found arsenic on the sample of turkey."

Emma's eyes opened. "Found *what?*"

Suddenly, Lenny cracked open. "*There,*" he shouted. "It's proof. You've been poisoning me. To *make* me lose weight even though I never *wanted* to. You always do what *you* want and you don't care what anybody else feels or thinks or wants. And this time you've gone too far. Cory and I are getting out of here. We're going to my parents'. Mom and Dad are waiting for me to call. I can't stay in this house another minute. You're *poisoning* me."

He was in front of her, waving the index fingers of both hands like a pair of six-shooters.

His forcefulness made him seem a foot taller. He spun to the shadows at the end of the room. "Come on, Cory," he shouted. "Grandma and Grandpa are waiting outside. Get your games console and some clothes. We'll pick up the rest of your stuff later."

I looked into the shadows at Cory.

Shirley was wide-eyed at being, for once, part of a scene that was even weirder than the one inside his head.

No one moved.

So I said, "However…"

12

What kind of private detective was I? The kind who puts two and two together and isn't discouraged if at first he makes five.

I drew a printed copy of Luci's email from my jacket pocket. Not a six-shooter, but…

Lenny cued me. "However *what*?"

"Later this afternoon the technician at the lab called me back."

"There *was* arsenic on the turkey," Lenny shouted. "There *was*."

"You need to sit and be quiet too," I told him.

Instant response. Maybe forceful-me could become king of the world and impose peace on earth and food for everyone.

I said, "My lab technician completed a range of tests on the samples even after she found arsenic on the turkey."

"I did *not* put arsenic on any damn turkey," Emma said. "If I'd wanted to kill him he would have been dead years ago."

I stepped toward her. "I'm not going to *tell* you to keep quiet again." Was I dangerous? She seemed to think so. She closed her mouth.

I said, "The remaining tests did not reveal any more poisons. However… In the diet lemonade my technician found a chemical that shouldn't have been there. It's one of a class of drugs known as lipase inhibitors. Lipase inhibitors significantly reduce the absorption of fat. Which is to say, they cause weight-loss."

Now *everyone* looked shocked.

But I still had the floor. And I'd found a new answer to the two-plus-two connundrum. I'm *that* kind of detective.

I turned to Emma. "You lost weight quickly from the start of this diet, yes?"

She nodded.

"Did you supplement your diet by taking a weight-loss drug?"

She hesitated. Was she thinking about denying it?

"And did you tell Lenny that's what you were doing? Or did you pretend your success was just down to salad and willpower?" I glared. "Speak."

"He never asked me. So it wasn't a lie."

Lenny's red face nearly burst into flame. "All that bull about self-control was…"

"Bull?" I offered.

"I'd gotten fat," Emma said. "I was doing whatever I had to do. Which is more than Leonard did. He never does *anything*. And *then* he cheated."

"So," I said, "you began to supplement his lemonade."

"Absolutely not," Emma said. "Ab-so-lute-ly not."

"Lenny, did you?"

"No way. I didn't want to *be* on the diet."

There was another moment of quiet.

Out of the shadows a dark figure stepped forward. "I did it," Cory said. He was in tears.

13

"This Fat Lenny puts arsenic on his *own* food?" Katerina was incredulous.

So were we all.

"That's exactly what he did," Shirley said.

When we left the night before, Shirley and I agreed to meet in the morning. He chose the luncheonette. And at ten-thirty Katerina was the only other person there. She even sat with us.

"He did it," Shirley continued, "so he could accuse his wife of feeding him the arsenic and that way get custody of their son."

"He sounds like a crazy, this Fat Lenny."

I was bound by client confidentiality so I couldn't contribute much to the discussion. But Shirley was subject to no such restriction.

"So he accuses *her* of false poison?" Katerina said. "This is stupid as well as crazy. Where is her poison bottle? Where are her fingerprints? How can he do such a stupid?"

"He wanted to take their son and live with his parents. But his lawyer said the only sure way to get custody was to show that the boy's mother was dangerous and unfit."

I doubted that Lenny would be meeting his lawyer this morning. When Shirley and I left the night before both Lenny and Emma were in tears, united in trying to console the grief-stricken Cory.

"It was the son," Shirley said, "who put a diet drug in his father's drink."

"Crazy runs in this family," Katerina said unforgivingly. "But it explains the weight without exercise." She waved a finger at me. "I said to you, there must be reason."

"You did, indeed."

Shirley continued. "And the son did it because he was so upset when his parents fought about the diet. He *hated* it. So when he found the weight-loss drug in his mother's medicine cabinet he began to spike his father's drinks with it. His father lost weight. His mother was happy. The boy thought things would work out."

"What is this 'spike'?"

"It means he put the drug into the father's drink without his father knowing."

"But why 'spike'? Spike is a sharp and pointy thing, yes?"

"I don't know why they say a drink has been spiked," Shirley said.

"Or is this boy *making* a 'point'?" She shook her head. "So what happens now to this crazy son?"

"Last night," Shirley said, "they said they would get some family therapy."

"You will find therapy for Crazy Fat Lenny and his crazy family?"

"I texted him three names and numbers this morning," Shirley said with an insouciant shrug. "It's what I do."

Katerina nodded approvingly. Then she turned to me. "But why does Crazy Fat Lenny choose *arsenic?* It is nasty bad poison."

"It was because of Napoleon," I said. "Do you know who Napoleon was?"

She glared. "French man with funny hat who thinks he can rule Russia and Ukraine. But he learns lesson."

"Many people think Napoleon died from arsenic poisoning because before he died he became very thin and arsenic can cause that. Lenny studied Napoleon in college and he said he got the idea when he found arsenic at his parents' farm."

In the same conversation I'd asked him what part Rhonda had in his planning. He'd just looked at me as if *I* were the crazy. Score another arithmetic mistake for the detective.

Just then the door to the luncheonette opened. The homeless guy from the day before entered. Shirley got up. "Hi Jan."

"Hi Shirley," the homeless guy said.

Shirley turned to Katerina. "Give him a good meal, on me. OK?"

Katerina said, "This homeless you help at your refuge?"

"He came in yesterday," Shirley said. "It's what I do." He was on an all-out courting offensive.

Katerina rose.

"The snow's about stopped," Jan said. "I heard someone say how rain will wash it all away in few days and before we know it it'll be spring."

"Before we wash and spring, you sit. Again coffee?"

Jan replied with a big smile and carried his knapsack to a table across the room. Katerina went to get the coffee.

I leaned forward when she was out of earshot. "You've been drooling over Katerina ever since you met her, Shirley. Learn a lesson. Lenny lived with a woman for *years* without speaking his mind or standing up for what he wanted. And he drove himself crazy—no sane man would have come up with the plan he did. Learn from that. If you've got something on your mind, speak up. Take the risk."

He looked longingly across the room.

Eventually Katerina came back to our table but didn't sit. Shirley cleared his throat. "Katerina..."

"That is me."

"I was wondering..."

"At last," she said. "I waiting."

A QUESTION OF FATHERS

It was Spring and the day'd had enough warm sun to promise relief from winter but not so much that it reminded of summer infernos. Just a lovely day. I'd walked in it. I'd savored it. I'd invited my daughter to dinner. She'd accepted. It was Spring. It was promise. It was future.

It's important to grasp good things. Not because I'm not as young as I used to be – was I ever? Or because global warming will likely bring perpetual cold to Indianapolis as an irony. It's because Life throws more than curveballs, fastballs or even changeups. Sometimes it throws down and out knucklers to wobble in your face and be impossible to bat away no matter how much you maybe want to.

The point was proved after the sun went down. Sam mixed her last forkful of spaghetti with her last leaves of salad and asked the knuckleball question. "Daddy, why don't you ever talk about your father?"

"Don't I?"

"Grandma does sometimes, and there are still people who come in to the luncheonette who do. But never you."

"I guess the subject doesn't come up."

"You must think about him. He was your *father.*"

She stared at me across the little table in the residential part of my accommodations. I said, "There's more spaghetti."

She pushed her plate away. "He has to have been important to you. And it's not like he split up the marriage or left Grandma."

"You don't call dying leaving?"

"You know what I mean."

"Sure, he was around while I was growing up. And, yes, we played catch and went to baseball games. But he died, and it was a long time ago, and I don't think about him." Which was true, if not that simple.

"How old were you when he died?" Sam asked.

"Nineteen."

"And it was a heart attack?"

"It was sudden and unexpected but I wasn't here and never saw the death certificate."

"You were in college, weren't you?"

"A sophomore."

"And you dropped out to come back and help Grandma with the luncheonette?"

"It had only just opened and her financial future depended on it. If the business had failed she couldn't have coped. His death was already very traumatic for her."

"That's what she said. She said, 'How he went, like that, it all but killed me, honey.'"

Sam imitated her grandmother's voice well but what I heard were my mother's circumspect words. "When did she say that?"

"Last week. I stopped in and we got to looking through old pictures. Why have you and I never looked through old pictures?"

"I don't think I have any that Mom doesn't have."

"But you're a photographer."

"Hardly."

"C'mon, Daddy. When I was a kid you used to send me lots of pictures you took around town. Odd things you saw in the gutters, benches in funny places and gnarly trees."

"You were my far-away child and I wanted to entertain you. But I only got into camera work because I'm a detective and it's useful for the job sometimes. That don't hardly make me no photo-grapher, ma'am."

"I loved the pictures you sent. And the little stories. And poems."

I stood and picked up her plate. "I have ice cream."

She shook her head, then looked at her watch. "I don't have time for you to tell me all about your father now anyway."

"Thanks for coming over to eat with *your* ol' dad."

"I talk about *you* with people," she said, getting to her feet.

"That's because people who don't know better think that being a private detective is interesting," I said, though I knew full well it wasn't me as a PI that she meant. It was me as her silly ol' loving dad.

"I don't even know what he did for a living."

"He started as a carpenter but did a lot of things. Later he expanded to more general building work."

"Do you blame his death for you not finishing college?"

"I went back after a while and flunked out. I blame that on your mother." But that story she knew. It had taken her to other continents but Life had brought her back to me and mine.

Did that mean she was entitled to know anything she wanted to know?

"This isn't over," Sam said.

I might have looked at my wrist and said, "My my, is that the time?" but I didn't have to. Instead my office doorbell rang.

She got up, holstered her gun, and followed me through to the office.

My daughter is cop. People who don't know better think being a cop is interesting. Unfortunately, sometimes it is.

Outside the door I found a bad penny.

2

I first met Curtis Nelson when he was a prospective client. Then he came as a victim. Later he brought someone else for me to help. Whatever this visit was about it wouldn't be routine PI fare. My work could be interesting sometimes too but, as with cops, that wasn't necessarily good.

"Hello, Albert," he said.

I looked at my wrist. "My my, is that the time?" I don't actually wear a watch but that wasn't the point.

"I know it's late," Curtis Nelson said, "but it's important."

For all his other idiosyncrasies, he is a client who pays. I stood back. He came in.

"Hello, Officer Samson," he said when saw Sam.

"I was just leaving, Mr…?" Sam's memory is not bad. She knew his real name. But she also knew that one of Curtis's eccentricities was to rename himself on a regular basis after child prodigies. Another was to claim that his biological father was an alien – the outer-space kind.

"Fischer," Curtis said.

I said, "Bobby or Carrie?"

"Bobby." He smiled. "I knew you'd know."

"He was precocious, I'll give you that."

Curtis felt that his biological "specialness" gave him natural kinship with the prodigiously talented young because maybe they couldn't be so gifted so early without having had an extraterrestrial leg up. By the end of his anguished life, Bobby Fischer might even have agreed.

"US chess champion at fourteen," he said. "A Grand Master at fifteen."

"And anti-Semite at sixty."

"Being different from other people can exact a terrible cost over time."

"It doesn't relieve you of the obligation to be a decent person."

"Of course not. But he was a tortured soul. And I can feel his pain."

I waited.

He said, "I want to hire you. By hire I mean engage your services for money."

"I'll listen to you for free, Bobby." I looked at my empty wrist. "For fifteen minutes. After that I have dishes to wash and places to be."

He went directly to my Client's Chair. He'd been there before.

Sam said, "I'll head on now."

"If you have time to hear this," Bobby said, "I'd be grateful."

"If it's a police matter you should go to a station or call them, Mr Fischer. And I don't get involved in my father's work. But if you can get him to say anything about *his* father I'd like to hear about it."

She left.

I settled behind my desk and took out a notebook. Miming the start of a stopwatch I said, "Go."

"My mother has died."

Sometimes my playfulness is not so funny. "I'm sorry to hear that." I tried to remember what he'd said about his mother, beyond her unusual choice of baby-daddy. "Didn't you tell me she'd been ill for a long time?"

"Years. So, yes, it was something of a release." He looked about to cry.

"That doesn't make it any easier for you."

"No." He dropped his head for a couple of breaths.

"When did it happen?"

"Ten days ago. But, Albert, that's not what I'm here about. Not directly."

I waited.

"It's my older brother," Bobby said. "He's missing."

"I thought you were an only alien."

"I didn't know about him, Albert," Bobby said. "I didn't know he even existed." More breaths. "He's my half-brother."

"She had a son she didn't tell you about?"

"I only found out in Mom's will and papers. I'm her executor."

"That must've been a hell of a shock."

"It seems Mom had Fitz when she was fourteen. His father's parents raised him."

I made a couple of notes. "Your half-brother was raised by his father's parents and you knew nothing about him?"

"The Mitchells. They blamed Mom. Mom's family, the Nelsons, blamed the Mitchell boy, Timon. I don't think they ever spoke."

"Is Fitz the name your brother was given at birth?"

"Fitzgerald Mitchell. Yes. And somehow, later in life, he and Mom must have reestablished contact. He even visited the hospice once. I don't know how frequent their contact was before then, but at the hospice they told me he called her a few times too."

"Your mother lived in Santa Claus, didn't she?"

He smiled, pleased that I'd remembered.

"And your half-brother, Fitz Mitchell, being missing, is that what you want to involve me in?"

"Yes. I need to contact him about the will but the number he gave to the hospice doesn't reach him. When they called to tell him Mom had passed, the woman who answered said she didn't know where he was or when he'd be back. Then, when I called the number, the woman who answered told me Fitz was missing and for people to stop bothering her. She wasn't his keeper."

"Did the hospice have an address to go with the phone number?"

"It's in Delphi."

A small town north and west of Indy. "Did you ask the woman what her relationship to Fitz is?"

He gave his head a little shake. "She wasn't rude exactly but she didn't want to talk. She sounded… like she was New-Agey, burning incense, and wearing a diaphanous muumuu."

"She *sounded* like that?"

"I'm very empathetic, Albert. It is something I was born with."

"You empathized a muumuu but not her relationship to Fitz?" I suddenly felt tired. "When did you call her?"

"Yesterday."

"So you haven't driven to Delphi?"

"I just don't have the time, between the refuge and other things to do with Mom's estate."

"How's the refuge going?"

"Oh Albert, there are *so* many people in this city who need help with their lives. I don't look for them, but they keep finding me."

Curtis might change his name with the seasons but one constant about Bobby-Shirley-Wolfgang-LeBron was a commitment to helping people, especially those he described as invisible to others. Maybe because he'd grown up invisible too.

"You don't have time to find Fitz so that's what you want me to do?"

"The estate needs to contact him, because he's mentioned in the will."

"So it's the estate that would be hiring me?"

"Yes."

"Has the estate got any money?"

"The estate is loaded, Albert. My mother owned property that is worth millions."

Bobby left a small but welcome sample of the estate's resources as a retainer. He also gave me free rein to do whatever I felt necessary. He'd done nothing himself beyond call Ms Muumuu.

The estate might need to locate Fitz Mitchell but Bobby's attitude was mixed at best. I divined this less from my powers of empathy than by asking him what he wanted me to do if I did locate his half-brother.

"Tell him that our mother has died and get an address where I can write to him as executor of the estate."

"You don't want, say, to tell him about funeral arrangements?"

"The funeral took place three days ago."

"And you didn't call his contact number until yesterday?"

"The hospice left a message with the woman about the funeral."

"Well, what about arranging to meet him? Getting to know him?"

"Just let me know where he is, please, Albert. He's got some money coming."

"A lot?"

"Half."

"Of millions? Good heavens." Then I asked, "What's the date on the will?"

He smiled. "Mom wrote a new will about a month ago."

"What was her mental condition a month ago?" Or ever, if she claimed to have had a child with an extraterrestrial?

"I'm not going to contest the will, Albert. It's what she wanted."

"Well, what happens to the money if Fitz turns out to be dead?"

"Why would he be dead?"

"Missing people sometimes are."

"If he was already dead when Mom died then his share comes to me."

"Did you kill your half-brother, Bobby?"

3

He didn't stick around long after that. The time on the stopwatch had run out anyway. And I had routine work that needed to be done once I washed the dishes. But having a fresh check in my hands was not routine. It lured me into thinking how to go about the new case.

Call Ms Muumuu? But it was late and she'd already shown herself to be hostile about Fitz enquiries. If she refused to talk to me I preferred she do it face-to-face.

So instead I floated around the internet trying to find information about Fitzgerald Mitchell. There wasn't any. No Delphi area phone listing. No memberships, no softball teams, no Facebook or LinkedIn accounts.

I looked up the Delphi Police Department. If I got nowhere with Ms Muumuu, I would ask if Mitchell was known to them. I learned that seven officers undertook to enforce state law and that people could apply to them for permits for handguns. I wrote down the address.

Browsing Delphi more generally revealed it was a county seat with a population just shy of three thousand. Nearly two-hundred years old, its claims to fame were a connection to the Wabash & Erie Canal, a huge corncob processing mill, and a restored Nineteenth Century opera house that in its heyday had hosted entertainment ranging from a Parisian opera singer to the Hoosier dialect poet, James Whitcomb Riley.

It was hard to convince myself that I was making progress. So I went back to the routine work so I'd be clear for a trip to the country in the morning.

But typing up invoices for law firms just doesn't hold the attention. I began to consider what to tell Sam about my father.

I *had* played catch with him, especially when I was single-digits young. And I did go to some ballgames with him. But he was a tall, dark and distant man. And his dying affected my life.

I *don't* think about him. Perhaps my brain protects me, after all these years, by blanking him out.

The next morning was sunny too. So of the two direct routes to Delphi I opted for the prettier one and spent more than two hours on the ninety-minute drive. Even flat countryside is beautiful in the delicious green of the new season.

My GPS showed the address that Mitchell gave the hospice to be north of center of Delphi. But if Bobby's empathy inclined me to expect the house of a New-Agey, incense-burning, muumuu-wearer to be isolated and an old church or converted barn I was way wrong. I pulled up in front of a fifties ranch in a small mature development of similar properties. The yard was plain and well maintained. A lot like its neighbors.

I got there about eleven. A large woman answered the bell. She was tall and broad. She was wearing a wreath of flowers in her hair. And she was wearing a green and gold muumuu. It wasn't diaphanous but I still shook my head in disbelief.

That was not the best body language with which to introduce myself.

"What's your problem?" the woman asked, articulating the words carefully.

"Sorry," I said, "and I'm really sorry to bother you. But I've come up from Indianapolis because I'm working for the estate of Fitz Mitchell's mother. Mr Mitchell gave the people at her hospice this as his contact address."

She sighed. "I haven't seen or heard from Fitz in weeks. I don't know where he is. I'm not his keeper." She seemed about to close the door.

"Which you told the guy who called two days ago. He's the executor of the estate and the guy who hired me. But, please, give me a couple of minutes. We don't know anything about Mitchell and need to contact him."

"So who exactly are you?"

I held up my license.

She took it from my hand, read it carefully, and looked from the photo to my face and back again. "It's an old picture, Mr Samson."

"I'm just not ageing well."

She led the way into a living room. There were deep silk-embroidered cushions on the floor, rich velvet coverings on the furniture, and patchworks of different textures hanging on the walls. The overall feeling was of deep reds and blues, and of gold trim. No incense though. Maybe an alien's foresight goes only so far.

"You have beautiful things here," I said.

A hand gesture invited me to pick somewhere to sit. "I'm in the middle of something, so please get on with it."

I opted for a deep easy chair but perched on its edge. I pulled out my notebook.

Ms Muumuu dropped cross-legged into a cushion. Her movement was completely comfortable. I'd have put her age in the mid-thirties but despite her size she was as graceful as a fifteen-year-old. But I'm not good at ages. She was probably sixty with the grace of a forty-year-old.

I said, "And your name is?"

"Claire Jevens."

"May I call you Claire, or would you prefer Ms Jevens?"

"Do whatever feels right."

"You said you don't know where Fitz Mitchell is, Claire, but I need to find him because his name appears in his mother's will."

"He's a beneficiary?"

"I haven't seen the will. I've just been hired by the executor to locate him. Does Mr Mitchell live here?"

"He used to, but I needed his room so he moved out. That was nearly three months ago."

"Where did he move to?"

"He never gave me an address."

"Did he have a job?"

"He's a handyman. Jack of all trades really. Whatever someone wants him to turn his hand to."

"Does he advertise?"

"It's word of mouth mostly."

"Do you have a cell phone number for him?"

A shake of the head. "After he moved, he'd stop by two or three times a week to pick up mail and messages."

"But you told the man who called two days ago that Mitchell is missing."

"That's because he hasn't been in touch for more than three weeks. That hasn't happened before."

"Did you ask the police to list him as a missing person?"

She smiled to suggest that was an absurd suggestion. "Fitz wouldn't like me going to the police about him."

"Why not?"

"The answer to your question was no. Move on, Mr Samson."

"Do you know other people around here – or anywhere – who are friends of his? Or anyone who might know where he is, or who he might be staying with? Or places he liked to go? To eat? Or drink?"

"There's a bar in Logansport called Denzel's, or something like that. He'd meet up there with some guys he used to know in the Army."

"Did he see active service?"

"He had two tours in Afghanistan."

"Do you have any mail or messages for him now?"

"The only personal one was three weeks ago from a guy he was supposed to be doing some work for."

"May I have the guy's number?"

"He said Fitz has it, but it's Jasper Ross. Jasper lives near Deer Creek. I don't remember the address but if you ask around there people will know. The messages was just to have Fitz call."

"You know Ross?"

"He came here with Fitz once. I think he was in the Army too." She rose, in a single movement, in its way as beautiful a thing as any of the fabrics that adorned the room.

I stood too, more aware than usual of an ache in my back. "What's your relationship with Fitz, Claire?"

I'd expected her to say that he was an ex of some kind. Living with her for a while and then being asked to leave. Instead she said, "Fitz Mitchell is my half-brother."

My jaw must have dropped. I said, "His mother's executor is Fitz's half-brother," and hers did too.

She sat again. So did I.

Quickly we established that she and Bobby Fischer weren't related except through Fitz. Claire and Fitz shared a father, not a mother.

She also confirmed that the shared father, Timon Michell, was from this planet and an ordinary human, if being an alcoholic womanizer and a "damaged, uncaring jerk" could be allowed to be called ordinary. She said Timon had left poor Fitz to be raised by his grandparents and escaped responsibility by joining the Army. Claire thought that Fitz might have signed up himself in a forlorn attempt to resemble his absent father.

Claire, years younger, had been brought up by her single, abandoned mother in Delphi. Fitz first came to the area when he was on leave because he thought his father might still live nearby. She didn't know how he'd traced their father to Delphi and she hadn't met Fitz until then. She couldn't help him find Timon.

"Timon's missing too?" I asked.

"I hope so," she said. "It's only Fitz who wants to find him."

"Wouldn't his – and your – grandparents in Santa Claus be likely to know where he was?"

A shake of the head dismissed this as she said, "Timon hated them, Fitz hated them, and my mother hated them. Fitz didn't win any lottery by growing up with the Mitchells. They punished Timon for bringing the shame of a bastard and then kept the bastard close so they could torture him. When Timon bailed to go into the Army Fitz felt it was his fault his father left. He's been chewing on that bone ever since. I know he also worries that his own dark behaviors might somehow have been inherited from our father."

"What dark behaviors?"

"Fitz is a complicated guy."

"How do you feel about your father's dark behaviors?"

"I'm not simple. But I'm also not missing." She stood again, showing that the grace of her upward mobility the first time was no accident. "And I do have something I need to do now."

"Do you have a picture of Fitz, Claire?"

"Yup." She tapped her head. "In here."

I rose and put my notebook away. I gave her a card. "If Fitz gets in touch would you ask him to contact me?"

"I'm sorry I couldn't help more," she said.

"Well, I wonder if Fitz's mother ever told him he had a half-brother. She sure didn't tell her other son. He only found out when he became executor of her estate."

"If Fitz knew, he never told me."

Secrecy and silence are the defining characteristics of some families. But my job wasn't to try to help the Mitchell-Jevens-Nelsons live happily ever after. I was just trying to find a missing heir.

As I drove away, I thought about the other places I could try for information about Fitz Mitchell. The bar in Logansport, Jasper Ross near Deer Creek, and the grandparents. But Claire had also told me that Mitchell "wouldn't appreciate" my going to the local police about him.

Recently I'd heard a woman say, "Tell a man not to do something and that's the first thing he'll want to do." It wasn't in real life. It was on TV, a sit-com. But that didn't make it any less true. I headed for the Police Department.

4

The police in Delphi share space with other departments in the city's Office Building and it looked a friendly enough place as I walked in. It even stayed friendly after I offered a uniformed officer my PI license.

"Up from Indy?" His nametag identified him as Dan Vomerton and he flicked my ID with his finger. "Don't see many of these. Is it real?" He pretended to bite it, like testing a coin.

It was real, all right, and precious.

Handing it back, Vomerton said, "So what kind of help are you hoping for, Mr Samson?"

"I'm trying to locate a man named Fitzgerald Mitchell."

"Fitz? Why?"

I explained why.

"Well, you won't find him in Delphi. Not now."

"But I once would have? Did he commit some offense?"

"Not in the sense you mean."

"Are you going to make me ask?"

"Fitz was a probationary member of this police force for about a week."

That was a surprise. "I'd been told he was a handyman. Being a police officer didn't take?"

"It didn't take."

I had a sudden image of a cross between Claire Jevens and Bobby Fischer practicing quick-draws and having his new gun go off accidentally. "What happened?"

"Chief Hillman came in one evening and found Fitz on one of our computers. He was searching police records without authorization." Vomerton sat back. "We like to give guys who come out of the services a chance here. We respect what they've given, and we respect how they're trained and we know that it can be hard for them when they come out. I went that route myself. But the rules of the job are real clear and when the Chief found Fitz taking advantage, he gave him two choices. Get out of Delphi or get out of Delphi."

"How long ago was that?"

Vomerton flicked through an open date book. "That was seven weeks ago tomorrow."

"His sister hasn't heard from him for three weeks. Might you, or any of your fellow officers, have any idea where he is?"

"I haven't seen him or heard tell."

"He gave you an address when he applied for the job?"

After pulling a file from a cabinet Vomerton read me an address. It was Claire's. He also read me a phone number, also Claire's.

"What did you think of Fitz, personally?"

Vomerton tilted his head. "It was only a week, Mr Samson."

I said, "Was anybody in the department closer to him than you were?"

"He was more Buzz's project – Chief Hillman. But there was nothing social in it. "Look," he said, "I can ask around over the next day or two. See if anybody's seen or heard of him."

"I'd appreciate that a lot." I handed him my card.

"But if Fitz comes into an inheritance, you'll tell him to remember us, right?"

"You guys don't run a charitable raffle or anything, do you?"

"Funny you should ask." He pulled a stack of tickets from a drawer.

Bobby Fischer bought a bunch.

"Some sick kids are going to be grateful," Vomerton said.

"One other question. What was Mitchell looking for on your computer?"

"Buzz said he wanted information about his father."

"That would be Timon Mitchell. Is Timon Mitchell known to you?"

Vomerton's face made clear that he was getting weary of providing me with information.

"How about some more of those raffle tickets?"

With a sigh he turned to a computer. It took him a few minutes, but eventually he said, "About four years ago we picked up a Timon Mitchell on East Front Street. He was drunk and abusive and firing a rifle into the air. Front Street's on the river and we've lost a few drunks down there over the years."

"Do you remember him or the incident?"

"I may have checked on him in the cells. I kinda remember a weedy old guy with long hair." He squinted at the screen. "The arresting officer isn't with us any more either. Shipped out for Alaska. Sorry."

"Did Timon Mitchell provide an address?"

"When he sobered up he gave us..." Vomerton squinted, then read me an address in Logansport and a phone number.

5

When I got back to the car I tried the phone number Vomerton had given me for Timon Mitchell. It was no longer in service. Fitzgerald Mitchell would have tried it, if he'd been on the Delphi police computer long enough to record it. And if he'd gotten Timon's address, he would have gone there. So I did too.

Logansport is about fifteen miles from Delphi and six times its size. But I found the address on the northeast side of town easily. And, unlike the phone, the house was still in service, a gray, wooden family home. It needed a coat of paint but the roof shingles looked pretty new and there were no holes in the porch when I went up to the door.

I gave it a good knock.

Nothing happened for a while, but as I was about to knock again I heard noises from within. Then the door opened, revealing the metal leg of walking frame. Then a hand. Then a tiny woman followed the hand into my line of sight. She looked about a hundred.

But her voice was robust. "Whatcha want, sonny?"

"I'm trying to locate a man who might have come here in the last couple of months asking about his father."

She squinted. Gave her head a single quick shake. "Whatcha selling?"

"Nothing."

She put her free hand behind her ear. "My grandson, Lewis, he don't like people trying to sell me stuff and he's big as a house."

I yelled, "I'm not selling anything." I shook my head as a visual aid.

"You want some cookies? I got coffee." She turned her back on me, swinging the frame in a surprisingly athletic motion.

I followed.

Eventually we arrived at a kitchen. I sat while she pirouetted between a counter and a table as she put a mug of coffee and then a plate of sugar cookies in front of me.

She didn't sit but our heads were about on a level. "Lewis works at a jewelry store now but he played football for Notre Dame. In the line. He's big as a house."

I nodded. I drank. I ate.

Then I managed to ask my questions.

"Timmy" Mitchell had indeed lived in a spare room in the house. But Lewis threw him out. Mrs Gates – my hostess – didn't recall exactly why or how long ago that happened but Lewis might. She didn't remember Lewis's number but she had it on the cellphone Lewis set up for her.

And, yes, another man did come to the house asking about Timmy not long ago. But he wouldn't eat any cookies or have any coffee and she was always suspicious of people who turned down honest hospitality.

My cue for another cookie. The sacrifices I make…

Events progressed at small town speed but I did manage to get her permission to talk to Lewis. Near the coffeemaker a cellphone sat on a charger. She hit two buttons. "Lewis?" she said loudly. "I got a guy here wants to talk to you 'bout Timmy that used to board. I fergit his name, but he ate three cookies."

I took over on the phone.

"Don't you be trying to sell that old lady nothing nor rob her neither." Lewis had a deep rumbling voice. He sounded big as a house.

I'd expected a Notre Dame lineman employed at a jewelry store to be, say, involved in security. But Lewis was behind the counter, dressed in a suit and handling trays of shiny objects. I waited while he talked wedding rings with a young couple. His touch among the rings was deft. He used his deep voice softly – not at all how he'd spoken to me on the phone. Lewis had sides to him. I liked that he looked after his grandmother.

When the couple left to consider their options, I explained who I was and what I was doing.

"That Timmy guy was bad news," Lewis said. "Dangerous."

"How?" I asked, thinking of his drunken, rifle-firing escapade in Delphi.

"Said he was good at fixing things so I let him do some work around Nana's to pay some rent. But then a kitchen cabinet he put up fell off the wall. Dropped down with a crash one day. No reason. Cans rolling around, flour everywhere. I hate to think what would have happened if Nana had been under it." His voice was not gentle now. "She called me and I took a closer look at the other so-called work he'd done. All of it crap, insecure, made of junk. Painted up to look good but don't turn your back on it, stand under it or put your foot down too hard. I kicked the guy out. Threw his clothes on the lawn, stood over him while he picked them up. He was lucky I didn't take him to an old quarry I know." He stared at me. "Y'know?"

I figured I could guess. "About how long ago was that?"

He gave it some thought. "It was springtime. Two years?"

So whatever had set Timon off in Delphi four years before was something different.

"Your grandmother said another man came to her door recently asking about Timmy."

"Yeah."

"My understanding is that Timmy is that guy's father."

"That's what he told Nana," Lewis said, "but Nana didn't like him so she called me. He was gone by the time I got there."

"Have you seen Timmy since you ejected him?"

He nodded. "Coming my way here in town once. He crossed to the other side pretty damn quick."

"How long ago was that?"

The big shoulders rose and fell. "Five or six months?"

"Any idea where he lives now?"

Lewis shook his head, then asked, "Why do you want to locate him?"

"If I find the daddy maybe the son will be there."

"Hmm."

I had a sudden intuition that Lewis might feel sympathy with a quest for a father. But fathers weren't my favorite topic of conversation. There were already too many fathers in this case. Or not enough.

6

It was lunchtime. I went to what turned out to be the Dentzel Tavern on High Street. It was at the end of a forty-year-old strip mall that occupied one corner of the intersection of a couple of Logansport's bigger roads. Two of the five other units in the strip had "for sale" signs out.

What struck me as I glanced around were the pictures covering the walls. Half were posed groups of men but the other half were of carousels, all horses and shiny shapes.

I took a seat at the bar. The bartender was maybe mid-forties and stocky. He moved easily around the area behind the bar, though he had a bit of a limp. I ordered a BLT and when he offered something to drink I asked for apple juice. Nana's coffee had been strong.

I said, "What's with the carousels?"

"It's all in the name," he said.

"Better tell me the name then."

"Dentzel." When that didn't clarify things for me he said, "It's a landmark in Riverside Park, up the road. A restored Dentzel carousel. 1885. The old-fashioned kind – ride around and try to snag the brass ring? Not many of them left and this one's a beauty."

"You're a fan?"

"It shows you can take something old and broken-down and fix it up so's it works perfectly and people can enjoy it again."

"Well, there's plenty about me that's old and broken down. So maybe there's hope."

"Always hope. That's the message." He gave me a smile. "You been in the services?"

"No. You?"

A short nod.

"That who the pictures of the men are?"

"Army buddies, yeah. And buddies of buddies. My bar. My walls."

I stuck out my hand and gave my name. His was Carey Garrison.

I said, "I'm in here for lunch, but also because I'm looking for an ex-Army guy. His sister told me he drinks here sometimes. I've been hired to find him because he's mentioned in his mother's will."

"Would that be Fitz Mitchell?" Carey said.

"You know him?" My eyebrows went up.

"Oh yeah." His pause gave the impression that his feelings about Mitchell were not entirely positive. "His mother died?"

"Eleven days ago."

"He said his momma was dying and that he expected to be a rich man. A richer man anyhow. How much does he stand to get?"

I shrugged. "I'm just trying to locate him for the executor. When did you last see him?"

Garrison considered. "Couple of weeks ago."

My eyebrows went up again. "Two weeks?"

"He was in here with his father."

"His *father*?" My eyebrows reached record heights.

"You seem surprised."

"I knew he was looking for his father, but he'd been looking for years."

"What's the story?" Garrison asked. "His father's actually dead and this old guy was a hustler who heard Fitz was coming into money?"

"Do you think that?"

"*Something* about 'daddy' seemed wrong to me. Crazy eyes? I don't know." He wiped the bar. "But they were in here for hours and really tied one on. I had to cut them off at the end, even though I like to give vets the benefit of the doubt. Guys who've seen service have a lot of things they need to forget."

"You didn't happen to call them a taxi and make a note of the address, did you?"

He smiled. "The guy they were with, I think they were staying with him."

"Do you know the guy's name?"

"Jasper? Sure, Jasper Ross."

"Lives near Deer Creek?"

"Couldn't tell you where he lives. He's old enough I don't have to check his ID."

"What's Ross like?"

"Well, he was in the Army with Fitz. Nearly lost a leg in a worse accident than mine and has some kind of pension. But he's pretty quiet – until he's had too many. Then he comes up with wild plans to make his fortune and goes around asking guys to invest. But I'm not sure he ever remembers the ideas in the morning."

"He was drinking with Fitz and his father?"

"I remember him being quiet, so I guess not as much."

My sandwich was ready. Garrison put it in front of me, then moved down the counter to serve other customers.

I stared at the plate, flooded with new information. After years Fitzgerald Mitchell had found his father. What must that have been like? Had it made Fitz more whole? Or was finding what he'd sought so long a disappointment? Maybe you have a lot more illusions about a father you don't really know.

Or a grandfather you never knew. Did Sam have illusions about Bud?

I realized that I needed to have a talk with my mother.

Before I left, Garrison said, "You really ought to go up the road to Riverside Park, and look at the carousel. You may never get another chance."

It was a gold and glistening decorated-cake of a machine, so wonderfully out of place in an Indiana park that it could have been landed from outer space. I figured Bobby Fischer would appreciate it.

I stumped up fifty cents and took a ride. My horse was white, with red and gold painted saddlery. While I was riding I felt like a knight out of a story book. All I needed was a distressed damsel.

There was something visceral about the ride. I felt what had moved Carey Garrison. There *was* hope for us all.

After the ride I sat in the Spring sun for a bit. And came back to real life.

I thought about the case. And realized that Fitz had picked a damn strange time to go missing if he was waiting for the call that would tell him he was about to claim his brass ring.

Maybe Bobby Fischer *had* killed his brother.

7

I headed down Route 29 to Deer Creek. I found an old-fashioned gas station which seemed a good place to start. The office was empty. There was a bell on the counter but it didn't work.

"Hello?" I said. Several times.

Eventually a young woman appeared from a room farther back. She asked what she could do for me while she rubbed sleep out of her eyes.

I asked for directions to Jasper Ross's place.

"Who?"

I repeated the name.

"Never heard of him."

"Ex-Army. Lives near here. I'm sure he has something to drive, so he must need gas."

"Sorry." She rubbed her eyes again. "Just woke up."

"Wild night?"

"A whole wild life." She said it colorlessly. I didn't know if she was making a joke at Deer Creek's expense or being frank and revealing.

I said, "Is there anybody nearby who knows everybody and their business?"

She smiled at my question. Then led me outside and pointed up the road. "White house, next to the corn stand. Ask for Milly."

Milly wasn't nearly as old as Lewis's Nana and she didn't offer cookies. Instead she wanted an exchange of information. So I told her my name and occupation, and that Jasper Ross had a friend who was mentioned in a will.

"Sounds like a scam to me," she said sternly. "What do you really want Jasper for? He owe you money?"

"Does he owe you money?"

"He owes ever'body money," Millie said. She spat from her doorway onto her porch.

"Not me."

"What's this so-called friend's name?"

"Fitzgerald Mitchell."

"He the old one or the young one?"

"The young one. The old one would be his father."

She squinted. "Comin' into money, you say?"

"Named in a will, I say."

She nodded. Then gave me directions to Ross's house, west of Deer Creek on the road to Camden.

8

I found it easily, a long narrow building that might have been a stable in an earlier incarnation. I would have asked but nobody was home. I knocked on the front door even more times than I'd said "Hello?" at the gas station. Here, however, the door was locked.

There was a green pickup on the grass beside the house but I looked first into the building's windows. I saw a room with a couch, a television, a table and some chairs. And a little kitchen. But the rest of the windows had blinds that were pulled down. Maybe Ross was asleep in his bedroom. Or having a bath. I tried the door at the back but it was locked too.

I knocked on the blinded windows. Nothing happened.

But turning away from one of them I noticed a rectangle of freshly turned earth a few yards east of the house. It was maybe five feet by three. Clots of clay rested on top, the only soil inside a rusting property-line fence that seemed to have been disturbed.

Maybe Ross was working on a vegetable garden.

Maybe he wasn't. I didn't like the freshly turned earth, or the fact that it was on the east side of the house rather than on the south side, where there'd be more sun for growing things.

Maybe my imagination was working overtime.

All that was left to look at was the truck. The flatbed was empty except for a few ropes. The seats of the cab were empty apart from a couple of candy wrappers. But on the passenger side floor I saw a large red toolbox.

The door was unlocked. I opened the toolbox. I'm not an expert about what a handyman's tools ought to look like, but the box wasn't filled with ribbons and fabric swatches.

I wondered how Dan Vomerton would feel about using the superpowers of the Delphi Police computer to look up Jasper Ross and the license plate of the pickup. I was sure Bobby Fischer wouldn't quibble about more raffle tickets.

I got my phone out. The signal was weak. But I didn't get to try a call because a gray pickup turned in from the road. It pulled up behind my car. I closed the green pickup's door and stepped away from it.

I was suddenly uneasy – an imaginative city boy, out of place in the country. We don't know what it's reasonable to expect out here.

I wondered what I'd do if a guy got out of the pickup with a shotgun. I kept a finger on my phone's 911 button.

There were two men in the gray pickup. The passenger was old and scrawny with long hair. He got out first. The driver was much younger. He was slower to get out. He was the one holding a shotgun.

They took a few steps toward me. The driver said, "What you looking in the truck for, fella?"

I had no ready answer for a man holding a shotgun. I stepped forward with a smile on my face. "Are you Jasper Ross?"

"I asked what you were doing in the damn truck."

"I was looking for something that might help me locate a man named Fitzgerald Mitchell."

"Whatcha want Fitz fer?" the old guy said.

"His mother has died. I work for the estate. Mr Mitchell is mentioned in his mother's will."

Shotgun man was about to speak when the old guy said, "Oh son. Your momma's *dead?*"

The nature of the conversation softened after that. "You're Fitzgerald Mitchell?"

"I sure am," the younger man said.

"I'm sorry to give you such sad news."

"We knew she was pretty bad," he said, glancing at the old man. "I've been meaning to go down to Santa Claus. But I didn't know she was *that* bad." He shook his head.

The old man put his arm around the younger man's shoulders. "Jeez. I'm sorry, son."

"You're Timon Mitchell?"

"That's me. Lornie died, huh? That's a shame. She and the boy was only just getting to know each other."

"I would have gone down again," the younger man said. "But I'd been looking for my father so long that when I found him I could hardly believe it."

Timon said, "If I'd of known you was lookin' for me, boy, I'd of sent you a postcard or somethin'."

"Well," I said, "I'm sorry about the news. But I'm here because the executor needs to contact Fitzgerald Mitchell. Can I have a phone number or give you his?"

"Give me his. What's his name?"

I hesitated over that. But I said, "Bobby Fischer." And I gave him Bobby's number. "Can I have your address?"

"You got the address here?"

"Off the mail box but not the zip code."

He gave me the zip code.

"This is Jasper Ross's place, isn't it?"

Nodding, he said, "How'd you know to look for me here?"

"Your sister said Jasper called her looking for you."

"Well he found me. Is Claire OK?"

"She's worried because you've been out of touch."

"Well…" He looked at Timon. "A lot's been going on."

Timon said, "Sure has."

I moved toward my car. "My condolences."

"I guess it comes to us all sometime," the younger man said.

"I'll tell your brother to expect your call."

"My brother? Oh, Mom's other son. I'm supposed to call him too?"

"He's the executor."

"But I thought his name was Curtis."

"He's taken a different name. He'll explain."

9

I wanted to put some distance between myself and the shotgun before I stopped to call Bobby. The next town going west was Camden. Traffic lights over the intersection in the center were green as I approached so I drove through. Then I pulled over, near a notice board with a poster for the annual truck and tractor pull.

"Albert!" Bobby said with enthusiasm. I heard crying infants in his background. "Where are you?"

"A little town up northwest. I've just given your number to a man who says he's Fitzgerald Mitchell. And I can give you a mailing address."

"He 'says he's Fitzgerald Mitchell'? You're not sure?"

"He told me that's his name and he gave me several details that match things I already knew, including your original name. And an older man with him, who said he's Fitz's father, called him 'son'."

"You found Timon Mitchell too?"

"Two for the price of one. They didn't know your mother had died. The older guy called her Lornie. Is that right?"

Sadly, Bobby said, "Yes."

I decided not to report that Fitz had bragged about his financial expectations. I wanted Bobby to make his own mind up about his half-brother. Having some new family when he'd lost the last bit of his old family could be a good thing for him, if he allowed it to be.

I said, "The way I understand it, Fitz had been searching a long time for his father and only just found him. He said he'd intended to go down to Santa Claus again, but hadn't realized your mother was so sick. Finding his father distracted him."

Bobby was quiet for a moment.

So I said, "Did you know that Fitz has a half-sister? The woman you spoke to, who lives in Delphi. Timon is her father too."

"It gets richer," he said quietly. Then, "The guy said Santa Claus?"

"Yeah. Why?"

"Because Mom's hospice was in Evansville."

We both considered that.

I said, "Isn't Santa Claus close to Evansville?"

"About twenty-five miles."

We both considered that.

Bobby said, "I don't like it, Albert."

"He didn't ask about the funeral either. But when you've had a shock, you don't always say what you should. Could be he'll have his head straighter when he calls you but maybe a DNA test would be a good idea before the estate signs any checks."

"Maybe."

I gave him the details I had. "But, Bobby, I'm going to stay up here for a bit, to tie up some loose ends. I won't charge the estate."

"The estate won't complain, Albert. Good work." He hung up without saying anything more.

I'd done work, all right. But how good it was had yet to be established.

Bobby did have a track record for empathy. And if he felt the twenty-five miles were important, I wasn't going to try to talk him out of it. Especially since I had my doubts about Fitz too.

10

Delphi is the next town west of Camden. I hadn't called ahead but I took a shot and went to Claire's.

There was no response when I rang the bell. This time I didn't walk around the house trying doors and windows.

There *were* things I could usefully do. Talk to Dan Vomerton, for instance. But first I had a question I wanted to ask Claire face-to-face. So I waited in my car.

And I thought about fathers, and about sons who went searching for their fathers, and about fathers who let their sons down.

One son had needed a father so much he invented an alien to fill the gap.

I sympathized with that. My own father was so unfathomable that he might as well have been extraterrestrial.

And what was at the heart of Fitz's quest to find Timon? To ask why he'd been abandoned? To dispel fears of a dark genetic inheritance? Or confirm them?

What do sons need fathers for anyway?

The platitude is that it's to teach them how to be men. I shook my head and made rude noises. I'd never have modeled myself on the distant opportunist my mother named her luncheonette for.

Is it different for daughters and fathers? I'd lived at a distance from my daughter but I'd worked hard to be a presence in her life. It's not like I wrote poems or took silly photographs for anybody else. When she'd come back to live close to me it was the greatest gift of my life.

But now she was asking questions about *my* father.

Timon's bad work hadn't killed anybody at Mrs Gates's, but my dad's had killed people. Two – an old couple. And injured seven more. I knew all their names. And I bet my mother did too.

There were others too, unhurt physically, who had bought apartments in the building that Bud, his delusions of importance swollen past all reason, had borrowed to create. He just couldn't pull together enough money to do it right. Not even close. He cut more than corners. He cut whole supporting walls.

Then, on a dark and stormy night, the building collapsed.

Bud had killed people. Then he killed himself.

I came home to support Mom. Helped her make what she could from the rubble.

Bud had incorporated, so the luncheonette wasn't lost. Mom survived.

And I found the time to judge my father for the self-willed blindness that allowed him to continue with a project he must have known deep down just wasn't right.

As far as I knew he never blamed himself or looked at his own nature. He killed himself, according to my mother, because, when his building collapsed, he was broke. Not because he'd killed people.

I don't come close to believing that all suicide is cowardly or wrong. But my father's was. A despicable and selfish act. A cowardly refusal to face the consequences of his own actions.

I picked up my phone and dialed my mother.

"Son? Where are you? What kind of trouble is it?" She was worried because I almost never telephone her.

Does Mom worry because she's afraid of *my* moral inheritance? Does she wonder how far my apple's fallen from my father's tree?

"It's not like that, Mom."

"What is it like?"

"Sam's been asking about Bud."

"She's with you?"

"Last night at dinner. Right now I'm upstate working, sitting outside a house. So I've had some time to think about it."

"Well, Sam and I looked at some pictures the other day is all."

"She mentioned that. And she said she's going to bring the subject up again. What do you want me to tell her?"

11

The sun was gone from the Spring sky when Claire got home. She tapped on the window of my car. I wasn't exactly asleep but I wasn't alert enough to have noticed when she pulled into her driveway right in front of me. I rolled the window down.

"I thought it was you," she said.

"Ms Jevens. Nice to see you. What time is it?" I looked at the clock in the car. It was after eight.

"You want to come in?"

She pointed me to her silky, colorful living room while she hung up her coat. I sat on the chair I'd used before. Then I made a face as she came in. No muumuu. No wreath in her hair. Instead, a long layered blue skirt and a darker blue sweater.

"What?" she said.

"You've changed clothes."

"I had my costume on when you were here earlier."

"Costume for what?"

"My next featured role as Electra." She took a little bow and then dropped gracefully onto the cushion she'd used before. "We're doing an evening of operatic selections at the Opera House at the end of the month. I have a solo." She laughed. "You thought I dress like that all the time?"

It didn't seem the moment to explain about the empathetic half-alien.

She leaned back. "I'd like to live life with a wreath in my hair. One less prickly than that one, anyway."

"What's stopping you?"

"My boyfriend, for one thing. He's a cop and has rather fixed ideas about how his woman should dress."

"Dan Vomerton?"

"Not Dan. How do you know Dan?"

"I went to the Police Department looking for Fitz."

"Tony got him a try-out. It didn't work. So… What's up Mr Samson?"

What to say? Where to start? "I believe I've found your father."

"Lucky you. Have you found Fitz? Is he OK?"

"I've found a guy who says he's Fitz."

"But you're not sure?" She frowned. "Why not?"

"I'm hoping you'll help me with that. When you saw him last did Fitz have a vehicle?"

"Sure. A pickup."

"What model?"

She laughed. "Green."

"Not gray?"

"I may not know a Ford whatsit from a Chevvy dingus but I know green from gray."

"What color was his toolbox?"

"Red. Look, what's this about?"

"One more thing. Did Fitz have a limp?"

"No. Why?"

"Because the Fitz I've found limps badly."

Fitz could always have hurt a foot in the last three weeks. But I suspected my Fitz was Jasper Ross.

The limp, the reference to Santa Claus and the fact that "Fitz" and "Timon" were driving a gray truck and not the green one all raised doubts. And I still didn't like that freshly turned earth.

Yet… Surely it was fanciful to think Ross might have killed Fitz so he could take his place and try for the inheritance. Big money was involved but big enough to take mortal chances for? And who was the "Timon" I'd met? A stand-in? Or would the actual Timon have seen some advantage to dealing with Ross over dealing with his own son?

None of it was clear, or made much sense.

With time it could all be tested. Questions could be asked. The garden patch dug up. DNA tests run.

But my line of thinking didn't allow time. I asked Claire, "Do you have anyone you could spend a few days with? Your boyfriend, for instance?"

She made a face at me.

"Or would you let the estate get you a motel room somewhere away from here? In Lafayette, for instance?"

"What are you *talking* about?"

"Just till we know whether these two guys are who they say they are."

"I understand that part. But how does it involve me?"

"If these guys *are* trying to scam their way into an inheritance, I think they'll see you as a danger to them."

"Me?"

"Because you know Fitz."

"Other people know Fitz."

"But not people the estate is in touch with. It was your number and address he gave the hospice. And didn't you say you've met Jasper Ross?"

"Yeah, but—"

"I know it's thin. But I'd rather be on the safe side."

That's when the door burst open.

"Fitz" and "Timon" both had shotguns this time. And it was "Timon" who led the way. "She-it," he said. "It's that de-tective. I told you we should of kilt him when we had the chance."

"You can't just go around killing everybody, Pa. You got to have good reason."

"Well, we got good reason now."

"We sure do."

So did Claire. She pulled out a pistol and shot them both.

12

Days later my life was finally quiet enough – and back in Indianapolis enough – for me to meet up with Sam and Mom. My head wasn't quiet but I needed to reestablish some version of real life with the people who meant the most to me.

We sat in my mother's little living room and I took them through the events that had followed Bobby Fischer's turning up at my office.

"You didn't know Claire had a gun?" Sam asked when I got to the end.

"I didn't know it. I didn't see her pull it out. I didn't see her pull the trigger. She told me later she got it when she hung up her coat."

"The gal was alone with a man she hardly knew," Mom said. "A man who'd hung around outside her house. Makes sense."

My mother loves her guns. I don't share her interest, but even if I had been armed I couldn't imagine acting as quickly as Claire had.

I said, "Her policeman boyfriend complimented her on her quick thinking."

Mom nodded with approval.

Then Sam asked, "*Was* someone buried in the yard?"

"Fitzgerald Mitchell. Wrapped tight in a tarp. They were going to move him far away later on, maybe down near Santa Claus."

"So the guy with the limp?" Sam said.

"Was Jasper Ross. But the old man really was Timon Mitchell."

Mom's forehead crinkled like a washboard. "How'd this Ross get Mitchell's father to come in on a cockeyed plan to impersonate the son?"

"It was the other way around," I said.

Mom and Sam looked at each other. Their profiles were almost the same. They were definitely blood relatives.

◆◆◆◆◆◆

"The other way around?" Bobby Fischer asked later. It was ironic that normalizing my life included the final report to a semi-terrestrial.

I said, "Timon Mitchell was living out at Ross's. When Ross heard Fitz bragging in the bar about the money he was going to inherit, Ross told Timon about it. Hoping he'd be in for a share, Timon engineered a reunion with Fitz. The reconnection began well but when they all went back to Ross's house Fitz's lifetime of anger got the better of him. He lashed out at Timon for having abandoned him. Fitz's fury set Timon off and Timon stabbed him with a kitchen knife."

"He killed his own son?" Bobby was shocked. "How damaged he must have been. His own son…"

Bobby's thing was empathy and when it applied to an issue of fathers and sons he felt the situation deeply. But he had a pertinent question. "How did Timon come to be living with Jasper Ross in the first place?"

"Because Timon was his father too."

◆◆◆◆◆◆

"His father *too*?" Sam's eyes were wide.

"I guess Timon never heard of condoms."

Mom frowned at me.

I said, "Then Timon convinced Ross that he was already in so deep he had no choice but to pass himself off as Fitz. Timon figured the boys looked enough alike for it to work. They could make up a story to explain the limp but Fitz was twenty pounds heavier so Timon had Ross eating more to put on weight because someone at the hospice might have remembered."

"How do you know *that*?" Sam asked.

"It's what Ross told the police. He survived. Claire says her boyfriend wants her to go back to the range. Apparently when you shoot someone it should be to kill."

"Unless you're good enough," Mom said enigmatically.

"So," Sam said, leaning back, "what they have is Ross's version of events. Daddy made me do it."

"It *might* have been Ross who stabbed Fitz." I told Bobby. "Maybe sensing a get-rich-quick opportunity. But my money's on Timon."

"Why?"

"The coroner said Fitz was stabbed over and over, a 'frenzied' attack. That feels more like Timon-gone-crazy to me. And Timon *was* first through the door at Claire's."

"Poor Claire. To kill her own father."

"She killed a man who would have killed her. I can vouch for that."

"But her *father*? And to shoot a new brother? *And* lose an old one?" Bobby was seriously sad on Claire's behalf.

"Maybe the bigger picture will catch up with her one day but so far she doesn't seem to regret the loss of a father she hated."

He shook his head.

"But look, Bobby, there's another issue."

"What?"

"Establishing when Fitz died. The Lafayette coroner reckons he was killed two to four weeks before what happened at Claire's.

If that window's right, Fitz died before your mother did and the whole estate goes to you."

"Oh."

"The estate should get an independent assessment to establish the facts as accurately as possible. To head off potential wrangling by Fitz's relatives."

"Does he have any relatives?"

"There's Claire. And Ross."

"Oh dear."

"And you can count on others appearing if there's as much money involved as you say."

He looked reflective. "I suppose the estate ought to know where it stands."

"I hope it does all go to you."

"Really?"

"You're a pain in the butt, and a nut, but your heart is good and you would do good things with it."

But what I was feeling was more than that. It wasn't easy to admit, but I identified with the alien's child. Not just that we both lived as outsiders but that we both struggled when it came to being sons.

"Isn't it sad about families?" the half-alien said. "They're supposed to be bound by love and held close but you can live knowing nothing about them at all. Even that they exist. And then you can lose them before you've had a chance to meet them."

"You would have met Fitz, wouldn't you?"

"Probably."

"What about Claire? She's not blood, but you are connected."

"Maybe."

"Give her all your police raffle tickets?"

"Or maybe more, no matter what the pathologist says." He smiled. "It's very lonely without a family, Albert. Look after your mother and your daughter. You're the meat in their sandwich."

Mom said, "You *are* going to get paid for all this work you did, aren't you, Son? Including for the time the judicial process takes and for the danger you put yourself in?"

"My client says the estate will cover my time and pay me a bonus. If it's not too big, I'll accept it."

Mom shook her head. She's never liked my attitude to business. But she turned to Sam and moved on to the next issue now that she'd said her piece about this one. She's done that all her life. "Your dad says you asked him about Bud."

"I want to know why Daddy never talks about him."

"Well, there are reasons," my mother said with a sigh.

"I know," Sam said.

Mom and I both looked at her.

"C'mon," she said. "Haven't you ever heard of the internet?"

"Then…" I began.

"Why…?" Mom began.

"I know the story of how his life ended," she said. "But a whole life isn't just about the end. He was also the man you loved and married, Grandma. And he was your father, Daddy. I want to hear about that too."

Mom burst into tears.

She and I had lived for a long time carrying a load we never talked about. Maybe we could never forgive, but I suddenly found myself wanting to tell my daughter about my father. I wanted to see my mother's pictures of him. I wanted to dig out the one picture I still had, of my father fixing the chain on my bike.

My own eyes filled. I wanted Mom to tell *me* about the man she'd loved. He might have ended as an alien in my life, but he hadn't begun that way.

AUTHOR'S AFTERWORD

These stories were all published first in Ellery Queen's Mystery Magazine, thanks to its wonderful editor, Janet Hutchings. Janet was also one of the people who encouraged me to collect them in a little volume like this one.

I began writing about Albert Samson in December of 1969 when I thought a story about a private detective who wasn't much like the tough guys of the day might be entertaining. He wouldn't own a gun, or beat people up, or womanize. And he'd live in Indianapolis, for crying out loud.

I grew up in Indy but by then I hadn't lived there for nearly ten years. There were other similarities to this "Albert" guy. I didn't own a gun, never fought except once, and was the married father of a daughter. Samson also thought he was funny. OK, my hand's up for that one too.

Shall I tell you about the fight…? I was in grade school – PS 70 on 46th Street – and it was in the playground, near a sandbox. It was me v Jimmy Boggs: referees out! Why did we fight? I have no idea. The only detail I remember is that I lost.

Amazingly, many years later, Jimmy attended one of my Indianapolis Central Library events and it turned out he remembered the fight too. But that *he* lost. How many times have you heard of two American men competing to have been the *loser* in a fight?

Looking back over my life, I've begun to feel I was destined to be a writer. I had some of the qualifications: I always felt myself an outsider and I played a lot alone. Then, as an eleven-year-old, I co-wrote two plays (with my neighborhood friend, Harold York: where are you now, Harold?) The plays were staged in my family's basement and my mother made the curtain. My sister played a murder victim in the second one. Even then I had to have a proper story.

Later, as a chem and physics major, serendipity led me to sign up for a creative writing class in the second half of my junior year at college. Over two semesters Alan Lebowitz teased out bits of what was in there – though never identifying me as anything special. Once – and I still occasionally remind him of this – he urged me never to give up science for writing. But I kinda had to, just as I kinda have to keep on working now.

This cycle of four stories ended when I decided to include Albert Samson's father. Unlike Albert's indefatigable mother, Bud Samson has almost never been referred to in the eight Samson novels and previous stories. I didn't even realize the omission until relatively recently. Well, now you know why he was absent. So do I.

These stories mean a lot to me. But I little knew how they'd develop when, going through my ideas drawer, I found a scrap of paper saying "AS has an alien client." Scraps of paper can be powerful.

October, 2018

ABOUT THE AUTHOR

Michael Z. Lewin grew up in Indianapolis though he hasn't lived there since graduating from high school in 1960. He's made his home in England since 1971, currently in central Bath – an outrageously beautiful little city.

He became a full time writer in 1969. His first mystery novel appeared in 1971 and he has written more than twenty books as well as short stories, and plays for radio and the stage. His novels and stories have won a number of prizes.

His daughter, Liz, and son, Roger, grew up in England and thrive in diverse areas of the arts. Their father is enormously proud of them both. His granddaughter, Aimee, is currently a physics undergrad (but sings and plays the guitar) and his grandson, Simon, is in secondary school and is, currently, an expert on the London underground and covers his ears when his dad plays the piano. Their grandfather is enormously proud of them both too.

Mike's sister, Julie Lewin, is a renowned animal advocate who lives in Connecticut and has written a brilliant book about how to change laws. Their mother, Iris Francis, became a social worker in middle age after a long history of social activism. She and her family sprang from Indiana. Their father, Leonard C. Lewin, finally became a writer in middle age and was author of the internationally successful social satire, Report From Iron

Mountain. He was born in New York to parents from Iowa and Ukraine.

As well as writing, Mike gardens on his patio, sings in a community choir, and tries to keep ambulatory.

There is more information about Samson, other characters and even the author on www.MichaelZLewin.com.

Made in the USA
Coppell, TX
20 July 2022

80198648R00121